THE VIRGIN SARDINE

By

Eileen Dickson
Elaine Douglas
Vera Morris
Julie Roberts
Eve Wibberley

Jeeve Publishing

First published in Great Britain in 2009 by
Jeeve Publishing
PO Box 2696
Reading RG1 9BQ
Email: jeevepublishing@aol.com
and info@jeevestories.co.uk
Website: www.jeevestories.co.uk

ISBN 978-0-9550522-2-4

Printed and bound in Great Britain by
Ridgeway Press, Ltd. Bramley, Hampshire

Also by Eileen Dickson, Elaine Douglas, Vera Morris,
Julie Roberts and Eve Wibberley

Fish Pie and Laughter
The Guilty Suitcase

We wish to thank everyone who helped and supported us

Front cover:
Elements, **an original painting in mixed media**
by Sue Tait
www.flickr.com/photos/suetait_myart/

Our chosen charity
Thames Valley and Chiltern Air Ambulance Trust

Contents

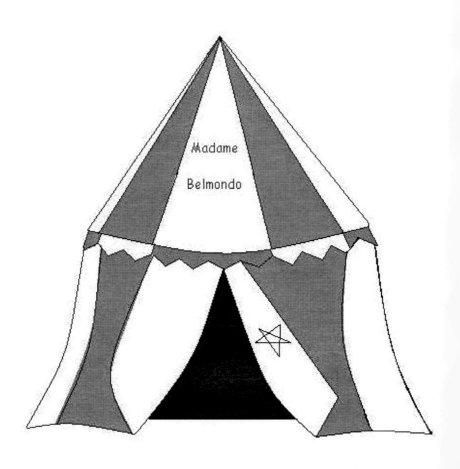

FIVE SIDES OF A CIRCLE

June – this is the time of year when a rash of fêtes erupts across the English countryside, like an infectious disease or a chain of daisies, according to your love or hate of them.

After another successful lunch at The Unicorn, the five writers, Julie, Elaine Eileen, Vera and Eve decided to spend the afternoon supporting the local school fête.

The playing field was filled with tents and stalls, pennants fluttering in the breeze. Pop songs blared from the sound system, competing with the hurdy-gurdy music of the carousel and the screams of a teacher, who had foolishly volunteered to be ducked at two pounds a time. A long queue of jeering school children, clutching their coins, waited for revenge.

Teenagers tried to win bottles of alcohol at the tombola stall, macho dads threw wellies and the cake and plant stalls were selling their wares like – hot cakes?

'Smell the fried onions,' murmured Julie, as they passed the hot-dog stall.

'You're not going to buy one, are you?' asked Vera, 'Not after the enormous lunch you ate.'

'I'm having some candyfloss,' declared Eve.

Eileen shook her head, 'The food police will get you.'

'Look,' exclaimed Elaine, 'a fortune teller! How exciting! I must pay her a visit.'

'Load of old cobblers, if you ask me,' said Vera indignantly.

Elaine quelled her with a look of disapproval.

1

The tent was impressively large, its dark blue canvas littered with glittering signs of the zodiac. On a blue board a pink neon sign flashed:

Madame Glenda Belmondo
Fortunes told
Tarot Cards
Psychic Readings
Spiritual Jewellery catalogue available
Member of MFTTU
All major credit cards accepted

'What's the MFTTU?' asked Elaine.

'Member of the Fortune Tellers' Trade Union,' rapped out Eve. 'I've had dealings with that lot in my previous existence.'

'Which century was that?' quipped Julie.

Helpless giggles from the others.

Eve bit into her candyfloss and eyeballed them as she munched into the pink froth.

Suddenly a woman shot out of the tent, tears streaming down her cheeks.

'Are you all right?' asked Elaine sympathetically.

'Of course she's not. Look at her. Can we help?' asked Eileen.

The woman clutched her hands to her flat bosom, rolled her eyes and wailed, 'Don't go in there! She's ruined my life! She's told me my husband is having an affair …' she paused.

They eagerly leant towards her.

'With the milkman!' she screamed, running away, waving her arms like a fiddler crab.

'Wow! What a story. Cynic or not, I'm going in. This I must see,' said Vera.

Eyes glistening, writerly minds whirring, they marched into the tent.

Madam Belmondo was sitting behind a round table which was covered in a velvet cloth; her feet were propped up on it, next to a crystal ball. Her skirt had fallen back, revealing muscular legs, liberally covered in dark hair. She was smoking a small, black cheroot.

Madame Belmondo blew a stream of smoke towards them, stubbed out the cheroot on the sole of her Scholls sandal, and waved towards five chairs facing her. She placed her feet on the ground and readjusted her large bosoms, *à la* Les Dawson.

'Please be seated, ladies,' she said, in a deep, sonorous voice. 'I was expecting you.'

They sat down in silence, taking in her coarse black hair, and the blue silk gown, sprinkled with sequinned signs of the zodiac.

'How can I help you?' she asked.

'We were wondering if you could do a joint reading at a reduced price, as there are five of us?' asked Julie dogmatically.

'Ah! A true Leo,' said Madame Belmondo. 'Does she tend to be bossy?' she asked the others.

They nodded in delighted agreement.

'That was a lucky guess,' said Vera.

Madame Belmondo's bosoms inflated to Mae West proportions. 'No guess, my dear lady. *Your* comment is typical of a quick-tempered and impatient Arian. Is it not?'

More tittering from the rest, especially Julie.

'Madame Belmondo,' said Elaine, 'not all of us are unbelievers.'

'Creep,' whispered Eileen.

Madame Belmondo, ignoring the aside, beamed at Elaine. 'Ah, a dweller in the house of Aquarius. *You* are full of warmth and healing compassion as you seek self-transcendence.'

Elaine smiled pityingly at the others, who pulled faces at her.

'What about me?' asked Eileen impatiently. 'What's my sign?'

Madame Belmondo heaved once more at her bosoms. 'You are a typical member of the house of Taurus: self indulgent. It's me, me, me. Nothing but me.'

'I say,' said Eve angrily, 'you can't say that!'

'Yes I can, little fish. *You* act blindly. You must learn to trust and follow you intuitions. In the house where Pisces rules you will be challenged to discern between illumination and illusion.'

Vera stood up, 'What a load of bollocks.'

'Stay,' cried Madame Belmondo, plonking a credit card machine on the table. 'You are,' she said, waving her hand at them, 'the five sides that make a perfect circle. The elements, Fire, Earth, Air and Water are all here. And you,' she pointed to Julie, 'are the Sun. That will be twenty five pounds. How would you like to pay?'

'I may be the sun, but I'm not an idiot. Twenty five pounds for being insulted. You can have five pounds. One pound each. Agreed, girls?' she turned to the others.

'So sorry, Madame Belmondo, but she was an accountant,' said Elaine, smiling as she placed a one pound coin with the other four on the table.

In the refreshment tent, after a good laugh and cups of tea they agreed that Madame Belmondo was the star of the fête.

'We should have paid her twenty five pounds,' said Vera.

'Why?' they asked in astonishment.

'She's given us the theme for our next book and a jolly good title for the opening chapter. What's more, I'm sure it's the head teacher in disguise. I'd know those legs anywhere.'

Vera

Fire

Aries

THE ORANGE SASH

The mad March breeze blew the branches of the trees, turning each one into the baton of an extrovert conductor. Inside The Unicorn, at their favourite table, the five women had finished their meal.

'Happy birthday, Vera.' Julie raised her glass and the other Babes joined in the toast.

'Thank you, it was a wonderful meal,' said Vera.

'Aries, the Ram,' mused Eve. 'You are a typical Arian, aren't you? Busy, busy, all the time …'

Eileen shook her head, 'And nothing ever finished.' The three other heads nodded in agreement.

'Thanks a bundle. I thought you were my friends.'

'We are … but you must admit …' murmured Elaine.

Vera shrugged, 'It's true. I get an idea, act on it without thinking, and the next minute I'm in trouble. Did I ever tell you about when I disgraced myself at primary school?'

'No!'

'I was seven, and it was my turn to wear the orange sash of monitor of the week. I would be given it at the end of school on Friday and on Monday morning I would wear it proudly across my chest as I collected the class register.

'I couldn't wait to take it home. My mother would wash and iron it and the sash would hang on the mantelpiece all weekend to be admired.

'On the Friday morning the teacher had equipped us with magazines and stubby little scissors, with blades as sharp as rusty nail files, to cut out pictures. No doubt she was looking for a rest before her exciting weekend of fell walking with her Methodist boyfriend. She left the room. I

decided I would show the rest of the class how my Aunt Ruth, a newly trained hairdresser, thinned hair.

'Chop! Chop! Chop! The teacher came back to find blonde curls, raven locks and ginger fringes strewn over the floor and crying girls sporting concentration camp haircuts.

'No orange sash for me. Instead disgrace and back to the end of the queue.'

'It all fits. Your element is fire, getting things going,' said Elaine.

'Usually in the wrong direction,' said Eve.

Vera ignored the last remark. 'Fire – that's a strong word. It reminds me of a story ...'

Arson at the Wheatsheaf

When I heard the snuggery door open, I thought, what now? It was after breakfast; I had cleaned up in the kitchen and the tap-room and was sitting by the window working at my carving. Mistress Windles, the inn keeper's wife, allowed me to have this time to myself and I was grateful for it, for it was the only time in the day when I could be by myself and do something *I wanted to do*; that is until I fell exhausted into bed each night.

It was the new lodger, Mr Chinnery. He did not go to work, and there was gossip that he was looking to set up his own business. He was a carpenter and joiner, like the other eleven lodgers; they worked in the shops in Covent Garden or St Paul's Churchyard.

I liked the look of Mr Chinnery: he had a plain but kindly face, a large nose and brown hair. He was of medium height but with a solid build, and his clothes were well kept and of good cloth. He had not spoken to me before, but had nodded and smiled.

'Good morning, young man,' he said, 'your name is John Falconer, I believe?' I nodded. 'What have you there?' He pointed to my carving as he sat down beside me.

I passed him my work: it was the head of a woman carved in lime. No one else had asked to see it.

'Did you do this yourself?' he asked.

I nodded again.

'Who is the lady? She has a handsome face.'

I swallowed hard and tried not to let my feelings show. 'I have carved the face of my mother, sir.' My voice must have given me away for he looked at me most kindly and patted my shoulder.

'And is your mother alive, my boy?' he asked.

'No, sir. My family died of the fever two years ago, in 1793. We came from Frome to London. My father was a carpenter and joiner and he brought us here to make the family's fortune. I had two sisters and a brother, all died - except me.' I had not talked of them for a long time and memories came flooding back.

'This is a good piece of work. Have you captured her likeness? Do you take after her?'

I blushed, both from the praise for my work and that I did look like my dear mother: the same golden hair, pink cheeks and regular features; they had caused me to be bullied in the past, but now I am tall and well muscled and can hold my own if someone makes a jest about my looks.

'I do take after her.'

He studied my face, 'You have shown much skill. You're the pot-boy, are you not?'

I nodded.

'What are your duties?'

I wriggled in my seat, for I was not used to talking to people. 'I draw the porter and cider, and bring it up from the cellar. I wash the tankards and glasses and do any other job that I am asked. Why do you want to know, Mr Chinnery?'

He paused, as though thinking deep, 'I suppose if your father had lived you would have been apprenticed to him?'

A bitter feeling rose in my stomach, 'Ay, that was our wish. I wanted to make fine chairs, with carved arms and backs, but ...'

'Can you read and write?' he asked.

I was tiring of his questioning; I could not see why he wanted to know. 'I can, and do calculations. I went to the Dame's school in Frome and my father taught me much.'

Before he could question me further, the door opened and Mistress Windles came in. She was neatly dressed, with a clean mob cap and apron and a kerchief around her neck. She was a hard worker and a good cook; that was why the inn's rooms were always full.

She looked at us as she stood in the doorway, her slight figure lit up by the morning sun, as it shone through the small window. 'I hope John is not keeping you from your work, Mr Chinnery?'

He rose, 'No indeed, Mrs Windles, I was asking John about his carving. If I have kept him from his chores pray accept my apologies, Ma'am.'

I swear she blushed at his gentlemanly reply and I inwardly smiled, for she had been good to me and I liked her, certainly more than her husband, who had a short temper and a ready hand for cuffing ears.

'John is a good boy and does his jobs well. I am sure he is grateful for your interest.'

'He shows talent,' he said, handing back the carving. 'Good day to you both.'

It was a busy night: the snuggeries were full and I lost track how many times I ran up and down the cellar steps. Most of the lodgers were drinking, I knew them well and many were kind to me, sometimes giving me small coin which I used to buy lime wood for my carvings. One I did not like was Jeremiah Smart; he kept apart from the other lodgers but often talked to the inn keeper, William Windles. They were not well matched, for Mr Windles was short and rotund with a balding head fringed with red hair turning to grey, and Mr

Smart was handsome but with a pocked skin and dark, hooded eyes.

The inn's doors were locked, the customers gone to their homes and the lodgers of the Wheatsheaf safe in their beds in the upper stories on the inn. I was in the porter cellar, which is below ground, cleaning up the spillages and lining up the jugs for the next day. William and Suke Windles were in the best snuggery having a glass of brandy each, as they did most nights, waiting for me to finish my work so that the cellars could be locked. I was bone tired and half asleep as I bent over to check the tap on a barrel.

The next moment I was pushed across the barrel, one hand pressing on my back and the other grasping between my legs. For a moment I was rigid with shock. The man was breathing down my neck and his hands moved to the top of my breeches, trying to pull them down. I let out a roar and pushed him off, swinging out with my right arm - he toppled back against the cellar wall.

It was Jeremiah Smart. Before that moment I would not have been able to tell you why I did not like him, but now I could! He leant against the wall, leering at me, his black hair across his eyes.

He laughed, 'Come, John, a pretty boy like you must be used to this. I will give you a shilling if you will let me ...'

I stood up straight. I am a tall and well built boy for my fifteen years. I clenched my fists ready to defend myself. 'I'm no bum-boy, Jeremiah Smart. Get out of this cellar or I will call the landlord.'

He laughed again, but not so confidently, 'I intend to have you, John. Boys made as lovely as you can drive a man mad!' With that he started to pull at his own breeches.

I did not wait, and while his hands were fumbling at the fastenings I landed a good punch in his gut and followed with an upper cut to his chin - I have watched a few prize fights. For good measure I gave him a kicking while he was down.

I stood over him, anger pouring through me. 'Get out of here, you catamite,' I snarled.

He looked up at me, blood running from his nose and he hauled himself up against a barrel. 'You will pay for this, John Falconer. I will get you in your bed, one night when you are asleep and then I will see you dead!' He staggered from the cellar, turning at the doorway and casting a look of vengeful hate.

When my anger had cooled, I felt sick. What should I do? Should I tell Mr Windles? Would they believe me? Smart had one of the best rooms, a single for himself and paid a good price. I too slept alone since the other pot-boy left and there was no lock on my door. The thought of him sneaking into my room and placing his foul hands on me was too terrible to bear. I decided that I would sleep in my clothes and wedge a chair under the door handle.

Two nights later I began to think that his words had been bravado, but I still wedged shut the door and kept my clothes on, apart from my shoes and hat. I was fast asleep when there was a frantic knocking at my door and someone shouting, 'Fire! Fire!'

I jumped out of bed, flung away the chair and when I opened the door I could smell smoke and burning wood. People were shouting and running down the stairs in their shirts and night-caps; I followed them, the smoke getting stronger.

Mrs Windles, in her shift and night-cap, a towel over her mouth, was at the top of the stairs leading to the cellar, from where the smoke came billowing up. She saw me.

'John, you are safe!' she wheezed, and then stared at me, 'You are dressed!' she exclaimed.

I blushed guiltily, for I didn't want to tell her why. She looked at me strangely.

Mr Windles came up the stairs, coughing, his face blackened by the smoke, and his nightshirt soaked in water. He went to his wife and put an arm around her. 'It is out, my dear.'

She sobbed against his shoulder.

Jeremiah Smart came down the stairs and Mr Windles turned to him. 'My thanks to you, for if you had not smelt the fire we could have all perished.'

Mrs Windles whispered in her husband's ear and he turned to me. 'Why are you dressed, John?

I did not answer.

He came at me and hit me across the face, 'You dog, you've set fire to my house! Hold him!' he shouted to two of the lodgers and they grasped my arms.

I struggled and shouted my innocence and then I saw Jeremiah Smart say something to Mr Windles and point upstairs. I stopped struggling and felt as though I would faint, for I knew then that this was Smart's work and he was paying me back.

He and Windles went upstairs and in a few minutes they returned.

'He is the culprit,' Windles shouted, pointing at me, 'We have the proof!' He waved some objects, I could see one was a tinderbox. 'Found in his room, hidden in the bed! Hold him 'til I'm dressed. We take him to the Watch-house!'

I was sent to Newgate prison to await trial at The Old Bailey. If I was found guilty I would hang. The warder told me I would be tried on July 20th, in fifteen days time. I have never felt so alone or so wretched. Even when my family died I did not feel so lost, with so little hope. I should have spoken up about Jeremiah Smart, but now it was too late. They would think I was making it up. I felt so low I could not even feel anger at him, all I felt was despair and shame that I would be hung as an arsonist.

The gaoler came to the bars of my cell and shouted at me, 'Visitors, Falconer.' He opened the door and led me into a small room; there seated was Mr Chinnery and an older man, dressed like a gentleman, with silver hair and a stern face.

I stood there like a fool, not knowing what to do, but glad to see a face I knew, and even gladder as Mr Chinnery smiled at me, 'John my boy, sit down. This gentleman and I wish to hear your story, but first I ask you, as I must, did you set fire to the Wheatsheaf?'

I looked him straight in the eye, 'No sir, I did not.'

'Why were you fully dressed when the alarm was given?' the gentleman asked.

I breathed heavy, 'It is hard to explain …' I muttered.

'John,' said Mr Chinnery, 'Is there anyone who wishes you ill?'

I nodded, 'Jeremiah Smart,' I said. Then I told them my story.

It heartened me that Mr Chinnery looked angry as I told them how Smart had tried to bugger me, but the gentleman's face showed no emotion.

When the gaoler came back Mr Chinnery gave him money. 'Do not give up hope, John. The truth will out.'

With hope, my anger at Smart came back, but as the day of the trial approached and I did not see Mr Chinnery again, my hope disappeared. The gaoler gave me better food and a bed of fresh straw – Mr Chinnery must have paid him well - but my appetite was poor - he should have saved his money.

*

I was scared as they brought me up into the dock. The court was noisy, full of people, the lawyers in wigs and gowns and the gallery packed. My mind was frozen with fear and I could not understand what was happening. The court was silenced as the judge, in a red gown, took his seat.

A gowned man stood up and said, 'John Falconer is indicted for that he, on the fifth of July, feloniously, wilfully and maliciously did set fire to and burn the Wheatsheaf Inn, in Red-lion-street, the property of William Windles.'

He then went on and on, saying how painful it was for him to ask for a person of such tender years to be punished by death for this crime, but that it was his duty, as it was the duty of the jury to uphold the law. He described in great detail what had happened. I learnt then that it was Smart who had raised the alarm, and that he had found the cellar door on fire with parts of an old shirt and burning straw used for tinder. The door post and part of the door were burnt through. He told of the evidence against me: a tinder box, steel and matches found in my bed and that I was fully dressed.

The witnesses were called: Mr Windles, Mrs Windles - who could not bear to look at me - and Smart. I watched the faces of the jury as they gave their answers. Fear rose in my throat and I imagined the judge putting the black square on his wig and sentencing me to hang.

Then I saw the gentleman who had come to the gaol with Mr Chinnery: he was gowned and wigged. A small flame of hope fluttered in my chest. I looked at him. The thin lips curved into a smile and he nodded to me. I looked around and there in the gallery was Mr Chinnery, he bunched his fist and shook it in the air, as much as to say, *Fight lad!*

I was called to give evidence and the gentleman led me through what had happened when Smart attacked me. The jury were leaning forward, I could feel their interest and when I told how I had hit him and laid him low, from the gallery a cry came: 'Well done, boy!' I swear it was Mr Chinnery. Many in the court room laughed and suddenly I did feel full of fight and indignation at the lies told against me. I saw some of the jury nodding as I explained why I was fully dressed.

Smart was called back to be questioned. I saw sweat on his forehead and Mrs Windles was glaring at him and whispering to her husband, whose face was red with anger.

The gentleman asked Smart if that was his real name. He blustered and the gentleman asked if he was not Jeremy Smith who was wanted on suspicion of arson and theft at an inn in Southall. Smart tried to make his escape but was grappled by the court officials.

A landlord of the inn in Southall gave evidence that he was indeed Jeremy Smith. There was a great uproar in the court and the next thing I knew I was found 'Not Guilty'. I was a free man.

I stood there, knowing not what I should do. All I could think was that I was not going to hang, that I would live.

Mrs Windles came up to me, 'I am mighty sorry, John, that we accused you of such a terrible crime. I hope that you will forgive us and come back to your old job.'

I was speechless, staring at her and quivering with many emotions.

'John will not be going back with you, unless he wishes to.' Mr Chinnery was by my side, he put an arm around my shoulder. With him was a woman, neat and well dressed, she smiled as though she knew me.

'Why, Mr Chinnery, what do you mean?' asked Mrs Windles, her eyes round with surprise.

'John has a place with me in my new furniture shop as an apprentice, and if he wishes he will lodge with my wife and me. He is a brave and talented lad and I have high hopes that he will make a gifted maker of fine furniture.' He turned to me, 'What say you, John? Would that suit you?'

I had been called a brave lad but tears coursed down my cheeks. One minute fodder for the gallows next a home and the job I had dreamed of. It was too much for me. I nodded my grateful acceptance and Mrs Chinnery, herself in tears, put her arms about me and they led me from the court.

On the way out we passed the gentleman who had saved my life. I wiped my face, 'Sir, I thank you. I was sure I would be hung.'

He smiled and nodded, 'Thank Richard Chinnery, for he paid my fee. He bought you the best defence he could. Prosper well Master Falconer!'

For my final apprentice piece I made a mahogany carver chair. Mr Chinnery came with me when I went to the gentleman's house to present it to him. On the back I had carved the signs of *his* trade: the scales of justice, wigs, books and gowns and on the back splat a skull and embracing it, the gallows' noose.

The gentleman chuckled, and nodded his approval, 'A fine chair, John.' Then he turned to Mr Chinnery, 'I wish to have another carver and eight dining chairs of the same pattern and quality. They must be made by John.'

My chest swelled with pride and Mr Chinnery bowed to the gentleman and assured him that it would be so.

Vera

Loving the Fire

The white walls were padded like a hot water cylinder and there was no sharpness anywhere. A watery, insubstantial sun shone through the window bars onto the iron bedstead, striping the cotton counterpane. Mary Borthwick stared out into the garden where patients shuffled along prescribed paths waiting for someone to tell them what to do next.

She thought it was about a month since Mother had last visited, but she couldn't really remember. It was better when Father came as well, but that had been a long time ago.

'They treating you well, lass?' he'd asked awkwardly. 'Bit stuffy in here, can't we open a window?' Her mother had shot him a look.

'Course not William, remember where we are!'

'Brought these for you from the garden, biggest ones I've grown since you were at home.' He held out a bunch of red and yellow dahlias bound in binder twine. She looked at him without responding, and he put them on the table.

'Bout of mastitis gone through the cows,' he said at last to fill the silence. 'Don't look as if we'll get all the hay in with this rain - mildewed like as not.' Then, desperately, 'Jet's had four pups, kept one, drowned the rest.'

Mary jerked her head up at this and opened her mouth, but he held up a brown hand to forestall her.

'Working farm, Mary, no room if you're not working, *you* know that.'

'You doing as you're told Mary?' inquisited her mother. 'Taking the stuff like a good girl?'

They looked at each other squarely. In her mother's eyes, Mary had never been a good girl.

They had left soon after that, and the nurse put the dahlias in a plastic jar. But she took away the hank of binder twine.

'Just in case, dear,' she'd said, 'don't want any accidents do we?' It was the only thing that Mary had of her father and she wanted to keep it.

Now she moved away from the window back to the round table. It contained some white drawing paper and a pot of coloured crayons. Angrily she chose a red one and began slashing at the paper. The red zigzagging spears grew higher and higher, and she coloured them in until they jerked off the paper onto the table top. She screwed it up and threw it on the floor to join the rest.

'Do you need some more paper, Mary?' asked the nurse padding back into the room on her rubber soles.

Mary shook her head. They would not give her what she wanted, but she could wait.

Borthwick Farm lay in an upper fold of the Sussex Downs. Its fields were stony and had broken both backs and harrows. Much of the hay crop had to be scythed by hand because the land was so steep. William Borthwick did this himself with an almost biblical zeal. Ideally, he would have sown seed from a bag slung round his neck, but even he realised that this was a step too far. The farm had been in the Borthwick family for generations and so had much of the machinery. Hesther Borthwick was an embittered woman, who thought that she was improving her station when she married the tall and silent farmer. A farmer's wife with a house of her own! She had not bargained for the long hours and hard work, for the little money they made to be sucked back into the greedy soil. And she could only have one child: a girl.

Mary knew that she was a disappointment. Had known it instinctively from when she was very small. They needed a boy to work the land and herd the cows, but more importantly, to pass on to the next generation of Borthwicks.

'If Mother can't have a boy, why don't you make one with someone else?' she had asked innocently at teatime one day. 'Ivy Hobhouse at the Post Office is very pretty,' she added hopefully.

'Mary, you go wash your mouth out with soap this very minute,' shouted her mother. Turning to William she said, 'I don't know where she gets her ideas from, honest to God I don't. Told you before William, that girl's not normal.'

William just grunted and said, 'Off to check the pigs.'

Another time she had asked 'Why can't we have a nice name for our farm? *Borthwick* is so ordinary. Ellen Elphick at school - their farm's called *Mousefield Farm*, an' they've got a dear little sign of a mouse with big ears on it.'

'Damn fool nonsense,' her father said. 'Our farm's Borthwick, everyone knows it without no sign. *Mousefield!* He spat accurately into the fire.

'Mary, go and feed the chickens,' her mother said, 'and when you've done that, go and clean out that rabbit.'

'I hate the chickens. I hate this farm an' I hates that rabbit!' Mary muttered as she stomped from the room. She banged the top of the hutch as she went past and made the rabbit jump.

Sundays were sacrosanct to The Lord, and to where He lived locally in the wooden hut of Northgate Pentecostal Chapel. Mary was made to attend Sunday School in the morning, and then again in the afternoon to hear God's Infallible Word and do Activities. Her parents had a lay-down in the afternoon and attended in the evening.

Goin' to do me own activity, Mary decided one Sunday afternoon. She had hoarded a bun and a bottle of orange squash from the kitchen, and was having a picnic with her doll, Betty Baz, in the hay barn. It was well away from the house so there was no chance of her parents finding out. It was dark with all the hay bales stacked close together, but she had a candle end balanced in a glass jar which she set on one of the bales.

'Would you care for some more tea, Miss Betty?' she enquired of the doll, 'Or perhaps one of these little iced fancies. Made them special for today.'

Passing a bun, she knocked over the jar and the candle fell out onto the hay. Immediately, a flame caught hold, tiny at first, then growing as it spread across the hay. Mary watched it, mesmerised. It was so beautiful, and it made an exciting, crackling noise. As the flames grew higher, it occurred to Mary that she should do something to stop them - Betty Baz might get hurt. She threw the rest of the orangeade over the fast spreading flames. They subsided for a moment, but then gathering momentum, spread on to the next bale. It was getting hot in the barn, and Mary realised with a horrible clarity that it was all going terribly wrong.

'What the hell's going on here?' shouted a voice from outside. Mary looked down from her perch and saw Joe, the farm boy who milked the cows on Sundays.

'I was having a picnic,' she yelled down, 'don't just stand there, get some water and help put the fire out.'

'Why should I help?' he said rudely, 'won't get paid nothing for it if I do - don't matter to me if the whole ruddy farm burns down.'

'If you don't help, I'll tell Dad you was having a feel-up of Becky Jones an' he'll tell your Dad and you'll get the strap.'

'Why are you such a nasty little girl?'

'Because I know such nasty people,' Mary spat at him.

When she was fourteen Mary was allowed to cycle to school on her own. Her father had lowered the saddle of Hesther's old bike and given it a thorough overhaul. The bike gave Mary great freedom.

The summer was long and hot, and no one was surprised that small fires broke out in the surrounding area. Bits of old tyres left on the road verges were easily combustible. A carelessly thrown cigarette from any passing car was enough to set them ablaze, as was litter left by the departing Travellers. Several dustbins also caught fire throughout the rainless summer. Then the school shed with all the PE equipment went up. Firemen from Lewes started to rely on their overtime.

Joe accosted Mary in the yard one evening after milking. 'Yer really loves that bike don't yer, Mary?' he said, looking her up and down. 'Seen you on it all round the place lately. In some funny ole places too.'

'What's it to you, Joe Howie? T'aint nothing to you where I goes or what I does.'

'No, but it might be to others. Better watch yerself, young Mary, else there might be some put two an' two together.'

'Then what? Go on, tell me, I'm really scared - I *don't* think.'

'You might just have to be nice ter me, that's what.'

She glared out at him from beneath the dark fringe with even darker eyes. '*Boys,*' she said contemptuously, 'yer all the same. *I've* got more exciting things to do.' She stalked past him across the yard, her fingers curled tightly around the precious box safe in the deep of her pocket.

Some thought it the work of the Devil sent to punish them for non-attendance. Others blamed the paraffin heaters bought cheap from the Quakers. The children were delighted except those whose parents made them walk the five extra miles to St Ethelred's in the next village.

'There's never enough coloured stamps to stick in the Attendance Books,' grumbled Mary to her mother. It was the only thing that proved that she had actually gone to Sunday School. The fire that had razed Northgate Pentecostal Chapel to the ground, however, had far greater consequences than a shortage of coloured stamps of Jesus fishing in the Sea of Galilee.

Joe found her in the orchard where she was lying on her back under a tree, reading *Tess of the Durbevilles*. Mary had been sent to look for eggs laid by straying chickens in the long grasses. Last summer's skimpy gingham dress was rucked up about her thighs showing a glimpse of white knickers. One strap had slipped down over her shoulder, and the brown skin was slippery with heat.

Joe came quietly up behind her. 'Last chance, Mary,' he said.

She saw he was looking at her breasts straining against the cotton material. He put his hand out to touch them, but she pushed it angrily away.

'Push off, Joe, yer smells of cows.'

'Silly girl you are,' he said, 'yer knows that *I* knows what yer bin doin'.'

'Go fuck yerself - no one else will.'

He stood up then, shook his head and strolled out of the orchard, whistling softly.

'Our Mary's been ever so much better these last weeks, don't you think so?' The nurses were smoking in their little room off the corridor. 'She's been helping me with the wheelchairs at teatime,' said one. 'Such a pity, young girl like that to be here.'

'Doesn't get any more letters neither,' said the other.

'Not that she opened them when she did, just scribbled all over them with those dratted crayons. So she doesn't even know that they've both gone?'

'No, s'pose not. Right, tea break over, best be getting round with the Happy Pills.'

They went out, leaving the door open. Only later did one of them remember with annoyance that she'd left her cigarettes and lighter on the table.

It was bigger and brighter and louder and more exciting than all of the other times put together. The barn went first, then the cowshed - she supposed the cows to be out in the summer fields still. Mary was glad as she didn't wish *them* any harm. Then finally, the house. Her parents were always fast asleep in bed by ten. She felt only a passing sadness for her bicycle which had been so much her friend and accomplice that summer.

Sitting on a low wall, she watched the flames red against the black night sky, a slight figure in a white gown. I will help with the teas, she thought, and maybe take the younger ones for walks.

She smiled and waited patiently for them to come and collect her. And finally was happy.

Eileen

Steadfast and True

Dripping with sweat, having completed the usual routine on gym equipment in the leisure centre close to his home, Bruce strips off and has a quick shower before putting on shorts and entering the pool area. Luckily there is a free lane and so he swims quickly up and down, smoothly cutting through the water with even strokes. After twenty lengths, pulling himself out of the pool, he goes to the changing room.

As he comes through the door, he meets his wife going out.

'Hello, darling! Enjoy your swim? I'm off to fetch Jake from nursery school and then I have to pick up some things from the cleaners and return these library books. Will you still be here when we get back?'

'Sorry, Fran, but I have to get to Heathrow by two. I ordered a taxi before going to the gym so just have to get my things together, but I will have some of that fruit salad with cereal. Any coffee left?'

'Be careful Bruce, won't you. We hardly see you now and when you are here time just flies. It's half term next week so do try and call Olivia and Rupert. I know it's difficult sometimes but they do miss you and love you to telephone. So do I.'

'I'll try, I promise. Look after yourself and love to the kids.'

Bruce changes into lightweight trousers, jacket and loafers upstairs in the master bedroom. He packs his grip methodically: laptop, change of clothing, razor and adaptor, basic toiletries, pens, notebooks, micro-recorder. Sorting through a pile of maps on a table, he picks one out and throws it into the bag along with swimming trunks and a battered old denim cap. Checking that he has passport, tickets, wallet and relevant papers for the destination, he places them in the inside pocket of his jacket along with sunglasses. Then zipping the grip he goes downstairs and into the waiting taxi.

The taxi makes good time and Bruce alights at Terminal 5 with time to spare. One good thing about living in Winchester, he thinks, it's not too bad a journey to Heathrow. He occasionally flies from other airports including private ones and, on the odd occasion, uses Eurostar. Glancing around the departure lounge, Bruce blends in with fellow passengers and joins the queue taking him to the plane.

Waking up in the centre of Istanbul to the cacophony of sounds only possible in a vibrant city where East meets West, where ancient and modern coincide, where the allure and the mystique and aromas of the souks tantalise, can only enthral the visitor. But Bruce is no stranger to this setting. He leaves the hotel through a side entrance and walks to a nearby coffee house, greeting his contact in the dimly lit interior. They sit at a table in the far corner. Later that afternoon, Bruce joins other guests at the poolside of the hotel, engaging in conversation with a very elegant young woman reclining in a chair which just happens to be next to his. His lean body, light blue eyes, cropped sun-bleached hair and determined mouth attracting more that a few glances, but neither he nor his companion notice.

'Hello, Fran. I promised to call, remember? How are the children? Can I speak to them?'

'They're well, darling. We're all next door at a barbecue. I've just come back for a cardigan. How are things going? How is Istanbul? Exciting as ever?'

'I've nearly finished what I came to do. Back in a few days. Anything you want from here? I've bought some souvenirs for the children. Istanbul's still a fascinating city. You'll have to come again one of these days. Love to everyone. Bye.'

Two weeks later a taxi pulls up outside the house; sounds of laughter coming from behind the hedge to the side of the garage.

'Daddy! Daddy! We thought we heard a car. Great to see you. Come on, we're playing a super game of rounders. We're having a barbecue later.'

'Good to see you too, Rupert. My, how you've grown! Hello, Olivia. Come and give your old dad a hug; you too, Jake. Where's your mother? In the kitchen? I'll be back in a few minutes. Off you go, all of you!

Fran is in the kitchen making mayonnaise.

'Here I am, Fran.' He kisses her on the cheek. 'God! What are you doing, entertaining the whole village? I've never seen so much food. Hello, Maisie. How are you?'

'Very well, thank you, sir. Madam's having a lot of people over and we don't want to go short.'

'I'm only joking, Maisie. I can see you've been very busy. It all looks delicious. When do we eat?'

'If you like you can get the barbecue going, darling. Maisie will show you what to start cooking. I'm just going up to change. So pleased it's going to be a lovely evening.'

'Who's coming to this gathering?'

'Oh, the usual crowd and I've invited the new family from the end of the lane where the Robertsons lived. Thought it a good idea to introduce them informally. I'd better go now. I can hear someone arriving.'

'What a good evening. Thanks very much for inviting us and now that we've met some of the neighbours, it won't take us long to settle in. We may manage to fit in a party at our place before summer ends and you're welcome to come.'

'Thanks, kind of you, Derek. I'm sure the family will love to come but I'm off again soon.'

'Fran said that you were away a lot on business.'

'Yes, business does take me away too much. Must keep the pennies rolling in.'

'Oh God, yes. Thank you for a lovely evening. See you around.'

'Goodnight.'

'Oh, there you are! That's everyone gone at last. It was great having you here with us - a family again.' Fran pours herself another wine. Her expression changes and she turns towards him, 'I don't feel I can go on living like this with you away all the time. Wherever I go, whatever I do, I'm always on my own. When the children were younger it seemed different somehow, but now Olivia and Rupert need their father and little Jake doesn't even know you.' She moves to stand in front of him. 'People always asking questions, my sister and even my parents ... I just can't take this loneliness month after month and the secrecy ...' Tears come to her eyes as she confronts him.

'Fran, darling! I didn't know you felt this way. From the beginning you knew what my life entailed. I've always realised that our personalities are very different but thought we complemented one another. In many ways you're very lucky; everything money can buy, a way of life many would envy, a delightful family, friends and social life. Remember, in this day and age, millions of people have to live apart through circumstances. I'm truly sorry that you are unhappy, darling. Perhaps we can get a few days away together.' He squeezes her shoulder. 'Come upstairs and say goodnight to our beautiful children. I have to leave at six o'clock tomorrow morning so I'll sleep in the spare room. We'll talk again when I get back from Tel Aviv and see if we can sort something out.'

'This is the BBC Lunchtime News. Earlier today a bomb went off in a hotel in the centre of Tel Aviv causing a number of fatalities and many injuries. We hope to be able to give you more details later this evening'

Fran hears this news in disbelief. She spends hours calling everyone she can think of who might have some information. Terrified, exhausted and frustrated she collapses on to the bed when the phone rings.

'Fran, is that you? It's Bruce. I've been trying to call you. I'm OK; just getting on a plane for the UK now. See you early tomorrow morning.'

'Oh! Thank God! What happened?' The line is dead. 'Are you there?'

Struggling out of the taxi, arm in a sling, bandage round his head, Bruce rings the doorbell. Home at last in the peaceful countryside of England. The past twenty-four hours seem like a nightmare. The door opens and Fran gasps, 'You didn't tell me you were hurt!'

Later in the day, they settle on a sofa in the sitting room, drinks in hand.

'I hope you're going to give all this up. It's time to stop, if only for the children. *Please*, darling.'

'Fran, we've been through all this. It's the buzz. I love my job, meeting people and going to other countries. I'm a foreign correspondent. That's what I do and I just might make a difference.'

She looks at him blankly.

'By the way, I'm off to Thailand in two weeks,' he continues, 'how about going up to Scotland, the Western Isles, till then? Jake would love it and we can look up Anne and Hamish.'

Fran sighs deeply. Her head tells her to leave this man and lead a quiet life but her heart cries out, overwhelming her. There is no decision to be made.
There never was.

Elaine

White Island, New Zealand

'My God! And they call this *a scenic attraction?*'

After two hours pounding across the ocean in a motor boat, I am feeling queasy. We are fast approaching our destination; an active marine volcano which rises from the sea in all its awesome ugliness. As we draw nearer plumes of steam rise from the mountain ridge, partially surrounding the crater, and drift away in the morning sunshine. Such a forbidding island, dark and menacing against the clear blue sky. The stark outlines of the greyish-brown mountain become clearer. It reminds me of a broken tooth, half missing, hollow inside. There's no sign of ashing today so we'll be able to go ashore. I can't imagine why Captain Cook named it 'White Island'.

I had to come. I wanted to see for myself where it had happened.

Getting ashore is no easy matter. Wearing hard hats with face masks ready, we clamber into dinghies to cross from our anchorage. My turn comes. Standing in the bobbing dinghy, I grab the rusty vertical ladder and up I climb on to a rough platform. From there, I leap across to the perilous black boulders covering the shore and promptly land on my back. It's hard to believe I'm still on earth; such a barren place and yet the debris of corroded machinery and the remains of crumbling buildings surround me. Man has been here and left his mark. A sinister place. I am walking into the jaws of an active volcano.

Following in the guide's footsteps, the group makes its way, Indian file, upwards towards the crater-lake over rough terrain. The path is bordered by super-heated sulphurous steamy vents. They have slowly built into mounds and columns of yellow, white and rust-coloured crystals. More black boulders, like so many grotesque elephants, surround us. The smell of gas is choking. Our guide throws a rock on the ground and the hollow sound reminds me that the crust is thin and perilous in this extraordinary place.

'Please, follow me carefully,' instructs the guide, 'if rocks start falling, run to the nearest large boulder and get behind it. There's no way you'll outrun the falling rocks.'

Why did I come?

It's a hard climb to reach the rim of the lake. I arrive panting to look down into its green murky water. Steam rises from its surface.

'How deep is it?' I ask.

'Seventy metres below sea level.'

I shudder - whatever made them come here?

Sulphur had been the draw. Towards the end of the nineteenth century moves were afoot to mine sulphur from White Island for fertiliser, gunpowder and other commodities. There was money to be made. It would be easy.

Men were brought to the island; some took one look at the stark surroundings and refused to stay. Indeed, one soul tied himself to the mast and refused to move till the vessel set sail for home. Those who stayed built living quarters and the plant. Here rock was fed into retorts to extract the sulphur which was bagged and shipped to the mainland. It was backbreaking work to construct the rough roads from the quarry to the seashore. They relied on supplies from Whakatane, the nearest port, but the weather could be terrible and sometimes the workers had to fish for their supper.

The firemen, Matt and Pete, were mates; in those days that was all they could claim to be. They shared a hut and kept themselves to themselves. The other men left them alone. The miners needed their skills; otherwise they would not have been tolerated in this totally male society. They were essential team members should anything go wrong in the plant and plenty could go wrong. The highly acidic atmosphere on the volcano corroded everything; metals were slowly eaten away: tractors, rails, steel reinforced concrete, the hoppers, the retorts. Even their clothes rotted over a few months and their shoes had to be replaced frequently.

Mining started in earnest in February 1914.

Just three months later there was an explosion in the works; one of the retorts burst without warning. No one believed it could corrode in such a short time.

Matt was on duty and was severely burnt. There was no means of getting him to the mainland quickly for treatment. The men did their best with the first aid available but Matt died in Pete's arms later the same day. Pete was distraught. He had been fishing when he heard the explosion, but he was too late. When a vessel arrived the next day, he accompanied the body back to Whakatane. Although he contacted Matt's relatives in England, he was left to arrange the funeral and deal with Matt's affairs. He kept his watch but sent the rest of his belongings back to the United Kingdom.

Pete returned to White Island with another fireman, Bert, who refused to share the room with him. The plant was repaired and mining continued. Pete worked his shifts but brooded over the death of his dear friend. He became very depressed and spent more and more time alone in his hut; even fetching his meals from the kitchen to eat in his room. The rest of the men did nothing to encourage him to join them; as long as he turned up for his shift they left him to his own devices. He had never been popular, but since Matt's death, he'd become morose, bad tempered and barely spoke to anyone.

It was sometime in June that Pete did not turn up for his shift. His door was locked and there was no response to Bert's banging and shouting. Bert took his shift but then decided to force the lock. Pete was not in his room. He alerted the other men by which time it was dark and impossible to search for him in such a treacherous environment. Some muttered 'good riddance' but the following day they set out in two search parties, picking their way carefully over hazardous ground, their shouts mingling with the calls of gannets returning to their breeding habitat on the flanks of the mountain. Overnight, layers of ash had spewed over the landscape. It was like walking in a fine powder with no path to follow.

For two days they searched without success, coming back to the camp at nightfall, tired, hungry and covered in a film of ash. They thought perhaps he'd gone fishing and been washed out to sea, or maybe he'd climbed the perilous path up over the western rim towards the gannet colony and fallen

The following day, one shift returned to work and the rest decided to take one last look round the crater-lake. It was here they found, under layers of white ash, Pete's boots standing neatly side by side on the edge of the lake, but no sign of him. Had he, in his misery, committed suicide? Or had some one helped him into the scalding lake?

A few days later two policemen arrived. They took statements from everyone and left.

In September, the supply vessel was delayed several days by bad weather. It eventually arrived at nightfall, and anchored a little way off, ready to unload in the morning. The captain sounded the ship's horn as usual to alert the men on shore. There was no response. It was eerily dark; there were no lights showing from the camp, but nothing could be done till morning.

As dawn broke, the captain trained his glasses on the shore. To his horror there was no sign of habitation or life. The whole landscape had changed. The crew quickly lowered the lifeboat and rowed towards the shore, but there was nowhere to land as even the small jetty had disappeared. Eventually they waded ashore and stood in the mud and debris gazing in astonishment at the unfamiliar scene. To the south-west, the face of the mountain had broken away resulting in a volcanic landslide, a lahar, which had crashed down across the crater floor. In its path lay the sulphur plant and camp. The boiler house, the retort house, the kitchen-cum-dining room, the living quarters had all gone. There was no sign of the men. Had they escaped? Had they been buried alive or drowned as the lahar plunged into the sea?

Days later a rescue party arrived from the mainland. They dug through the steaming rubble where the camp had been hoping someone had survived. Nothing was found. Divers searched the slopes of the submarine mountain. They found boulders as large as vehicles scattered beneath the cloudy water. It was as if some giant had hurled them from the top of the mountain. As they were leaving they were astonished to see the cook's neutered cat, mewing, bedraggled and hungry. It had been called Pete in a cruel jest by the miners, but became known as Peter the Great in Whakatane.

I make my way on round the island with the group and down towards the shore again, passing craters, steaming vents and rocky outcrops, stepping over hot streams of reddish water, always wary of falling rocks. Back near the sea lie stark reminders of the last attempt at sulphur mining on White Island; the derelict factory built in 1925 on the debris of the lahar.

I leave White Island to its ghosts, secrets, grim past and hidden dangers. It is not my idea of a scenic attraction. Perhaps one day, centuries hence, it will be dormant, covered in vegetation and inhabited by humans, animals and birds; its growing pains and tragic history forgotten.

Eve

Summer Flower

I am Summer Flower of the Cheyenne. I was born sixteen summers ago when the sun was high in the spirit world above us, and the buffalo grazed on the great plains.

Today the sun does not show and the daylight is short and the nights are long and cold. I have around my shoulders a fur skin, pounded and softened by the squaws and traded by my father, Running Deer, as a wedding gift to me. For when the moon shines round I will lay with my man-brave, Storm Cloud, for the first time.

It is not a good time for our ceremony. There is much discontent and the elders sit smoking their pipes and discuss much about the troubles with the White Man. I hear my mother and the other squaws say we have lost much of our land and have only a small part left. This has been called an Indian Reservation.

Three full seasons ago, what the White Man called 1861, six Cheyenne Chiefs, including our Chief Black Kettle, and four Arapaho Chiefs marked a paper called the *Treaty of Fort Wise*. It gave much of our great buffalo plains away. The Dog Soldier and other Cheyenne Chiefs who were not there have been angered by the signing. They say we were cheated, because it was not agreed by all the tribes and they will not abide by it.

There has been much fighting and death, much distrust and hatred. Now we have come to Fort Lyon with Chief Black Kettle to make peace. The fort's White Chief told Black Kettle to travel north to Sand Creek. That a White Man's flag must fly above Black Kettle's tepee, as a peace sign and we would be protected.

With the White Man's promise, my father, with the other braves, has gone hunting.

The day is ending and the sun is leaving our world. Here in our tepee, my mother lies in a deep sleep.

Soon the night demons will prowl the land, hunting for any brave that strays from the firelight.

I do not fear the dark or the demons.

Since this summer past, I have been blessed with the power of the Shaman. If he knew, I would be killed, for I am a threat to him and his honoured place beside Chief Black Kettle. I do not understand why I have been chosen - a squaw of no standing in the great Cheyenne nation. But I have, and I must go to meet the spirits; for I sense a strangeness of my mind that is calling to be answered.

I need take only my hidden sack and fur skin to keep out the cold.

There are no sounds coming from the village. Chief Black Kettle must also be asleep; his mind has retreated from the turmoil of asking the Great Spirit for guidance with the White Man. The few horses tethered to the line are also silent; it is strange, for they neigh and shuffle their hooves when the braves are here.

The tepee flap was secured tight to keep the warmth of our fire inside, but it has not stopped me leaving. I pass two rings of tepees to leave the circle of light from the fire and I am now with the darkness and the demons.

I climb the earth slope, for it will give me sight of my Cheyenne people asleep and safe. Why does the thought *safe* trouble me? We have the White Chief's flag of promise. Perhaps it is because all our fighting braves are away – only the old and young ones remain and they have but the strength of a squaw – useless against an enemy. I must not dwell on this, my spirit calls and I must light a fire with the wood I have stored here.

Now the fire burns bright and the smoke is rising in the cold air. It is not yet time for the white covering to come and keep us in our tepees. This winter I shall be warm against Storm Cloud, hoping that our seeds have met and come the next summer, I shall bring our papoose into the tribe.

I have made a feather head-dress and a wolf mask to wear. I know that the she-wolf is to be my spirit. She came to me in my sleep, out of the white light, grey in colour and with teeth that showed yellow when she snarled and snapped at the birds I killed in my dream. I am putting them on now – there is a smell from the skin I used – but the spirit and I must be as one.

I have watched the Shaman when he has been searching for his spirit – he dances round the fire and calls with strange words for answers. I must do the same.

The smoke is thickening – now is the time.

It is cold, but without wind. I drop the fur from my shoulders and begin to dance. Now I must scatter the dried roots and berries from my pouch into the fire to release their strong scent that will pass into my mind and let my spirit roam free. I imitate the Shaman – shuffle my feet in half-steps, hunch my shoulders and dip my wolf-head and raise it to look into the smoke.

There is nothing there, only the drifting column stretching towards the blackness of the spirit world. There is something missing - I must chant words to call my spirit. Had I sung in my dream? I close my eyes and the words come - rhythmic and low. I circle my fire and chant.

My mind is drifting, searching for the she-wolf. I see her coming out of the light and out of my mind. I open my eyes and she is there, circling in the column of smoke.

'Spirit, tell me what you know? Tell me why I have this fear for my people?'

The she-wolf circles higher and leaps from the fire and stands before me. She raises her head and howls a silent cry, then turns and runs with speed away across the plain, towards Fort Lyon.

I do not know the ways of the Shaman after he has released his spirit. But I feel spent and tired, my mind confused. The white light has gone and in its place is blackness that is devouring me – mind, body and soul - I cannot fight it but must give in to its demand.

I have come through into the light.

I can see the she-wolf. She is waiting by the fire, her tongue lolling and her sides heaving. She has run far and fast. I am cold although the fire still burns. Where is my fur? I need it on or I shall perish like a flower cupped in the hands of an autumn frost.

I sit by the fire and the warmth is good.

The flames are turning red and my spirit wolf returns to the smoke and disappears.

The pale light of dawn is creeping through my village and it is as silent as when I left in the dark - no one is awake. The smoke is turning blue and I can see blue-coated soldiers swaying with the firewater that makes them wild and dangerous. A White Chief is amongst them. He is waving his arms, directing them into lines. They are undisciplined. Those on foot are loading their fire-sticks; those on horse are waving their long knives; they are all facing my village.

Great open-mouthed guns spit out balls of death.

My heart and head are beating with the rhythm of a drum.

The White Chief is pointing with his long knife and the blue-coats are firing and moving forward. They are firing on our tepees - but we have their flag flying! It is our protection.

41

The soldiers are not stopping. They are now at the outer tepees – they are using the short knives on their fire-sticks to stab the women coming out. The horsemen are galloping forward, slashing and stabbing the old braves, who are trying to defend with their tomahawks – but they are overwhelmed by the blue soldiers.

The village is a battle place. My people are being killed.

In the smoke the squaws and children are screaming, silent open mouthed screams as they run before the soldiers who are cutting them with their long knives – a baby is torn from its mother's arms and the knife pierces its tiny body, then she is slain.

The fire is turning yellow.

The blue-coats are burning the tepees. The young are crawling out, terrified without the braves and warriors to defend them. They are chased and caught. The soldiers are frothing from the mouth, eyes wild with lust. They slice the manhood of the children and defile the young squaws before the eyes of their mothers.

The smoke is changing to grey.

Chief Black Kettle is raising a white flag, the totem of surrender, but it is being ignored. Our chief is running - running with the old and children. All are fleeing from death. The soldiers are burning our tepees – our only shelter from the winter storms.

I cannot bear to look any longer. My eyes have been filled with the horror. My head pounds, my limbs shake and my tongue is swelling with thirst. To which spirit should I plead for this wickedness not to happen? Has the Shaman seen the same? I curse this power I have been given - that I must sit here and know this is to come. That I am not able to change what has been shown to me.

It is to be.

The fire is dying to ash.

My heart is torn into fragments, each piece crying for a dead soul who will lie on the cold earth. My pain is so great that I fear my body cannot cradle and hold so many dead. Yet I have been chosen to see this and to survive.

Why?

The smoke is returning.

The she-wolf spirit has not finished. Shimmering into being is Storm Cloud and I am beside him with a papoose.

Now I see my son-brave. He is not dressed like us, he is in the cloth of the White Man: long coat and trousers; a shirt. His long hair is tied like a horse's tail and he is holding a round hard head-dress. He stands before a White Man's building the size of a mountain.

Is this why I have been chosen? Am I part of the future, my son a leader of our people in the White Man's world?

The she-wolf is looking at me, her eyes locked on mine. She is beautiful, my spirit. She has left me with the answer to my fear – my people are to be massacred here at Sand Creek at dawn.

Julie

Earth

Taurus

GREEDY BABY I

'Shall we sit outside?' asked Eileen, pointing to The Unicorn's garden. 'It's your birthday lunch. The choice is yours.' Elaine magnanimously pointed to a rustic table and five chairs beneath an old beech tree.

Under a benign May sky they quickly surrounded the table and drinks and meals were ordered.

'I say, Eileen, have you been on a diet? You've wolfed your food. I've not eaten half of mine,' said Vera.

Eileen blushed. 'Oh dear, good job my mother can't see me, she was horrified at the rate I could shift food. I've always been like this, or so my family tell me.'

'You Taureans are said to be self-indulgent,' pronounced Julie.

'We have got some good traits: patience, determination …'

'How boring,' interrupted Eve. 'Tell us about your greedy childhood.'

Eileen looked grumpy, then she smiled. 'My favourite brother, Maurice, was on leave from the Merchant Navy. He was so handsome and at twenty-three he seemed to me, I was five years old, everything a big brother should be. My mother had baked his favourite pudding: blackberry and apple pie. After the first course of roast beef and all the trimmings, the rest of the family were distracted by an unexpected visitor, Aunt Freda. They left the table to greet her in the hall. They must have been away five minutes.

"Do come and have some pie, Freda," I heard my mother say.

'I tried to make my get-away, but it was too late. They stood around the table; my mother's face was a picture of disbelief and horror. Maurice laughed and Aunt Freda tut-tutted.

'All that was left of the pie was an outer crust and purple stains. I sat there with more purple stains around my mouth and a bulging tummy. I burped loudly and Maurice laughed again.

'I was re-christened: Greedy Baby I.'

The Good Earth

I sat back on my heels and look with satisfaction at the row of young lettuce plants now settled into the thin earth in their own little puddles of water. Prakash will smile and shake his head when he comes by later, yet another instance of my English foolishness, but I don't care. They are mine and I will nurture them as if they were my children. A flock of passing Bee-Eaters alighted momentarily on the Peepul tree, and I watch as their flashing green disappeared into the blue sky.

I love this time of the morning. The sun has not yet fully risen over the hill, the air is cool, and there is still a faint dampness on the earth. We are lucky here on the hillside, where there is more vegetation to hold the rains when they come, as well as firewood for the stove. They are *selling* it in bundles on Niwas Street! I was triumphant last week to have found a shop on Udaipol Road, where, if you didn't mind queuing, the rice and gram flour were several rupees cheaper than in town. Further to walk of course, and I had to dodge the *tuc tucs* and buses grinding out from the bus station, but, as long as I timed it for the cooler evening, well worth the money saved. There was a respectful cough behind me.

'Carrots, Madam,' Prakash reproved sadly. 'Or Beetroots. Beetroots is good for here.'

We may well be considered *poor whites,* but to Prakash, I was always Madam.

'Thank you, Prakash,' I replied, 'but Sir does not like carrots and I don't like beetroot. It reminds me of school dinners.'

We regarded each other with mutual respect. I would far rather have his school dinners of vegetable curries and nan bread taken in chattee tins, than my own plate of Spam, and butter beans with the beetroot juice leaking into the lettuce.

He shook his head over my little green plants and went over to his own patch of the garden.

Roland liked to call him our *gardener*, but of course he was nothing of the sort. He'd adopted us when we first came to the house three years ago, and I truly believe that if it were not for Prakash, we would have starved that first winter. Roland said he'd chosen Udaipur for our escape because of its cultural heritage. I secretly thought it was because he'd read about it in *The Lonely Planet - possibly no city in Rajasthan is quite as romantic as Udaipur*. In those days, I took everything he said as gospel. And of course, I wanted to escape with him. It was also the cheapest place to live.

Roland Firth was a lecher. Much later, when I was lonely and disillusioned, I looked it up in the dictionary; the definition is *one who freely indulges his sexual instincts*. That's my Roland, I thought grimly. The University, however, did not feel they could indulge him any further, and phrases such as *gross moral turpitude* were used at his Exit Interview. A little unfairly, I thought, since I was a mature student, but as they'd been looking for an excuse to get rid of him, our convenient affair served their purpose very well. I had sympathized with his tirades against *redbrick political jealousy*, much as I believed that he had money and would divorce his wife. Both of these I found to be untrue.

'Good morning, Mrs Firth, I hope I find you well?'

God, was it that time already - how long had I been mooning over the lettuces? Mrs Chatergee stood by the garden gate, an amazing picture in white high heeled shoes, matching handbag and shiny, navy blue suit. She looked extremely hot.

'Goodness, am I a little early for you? I will tell my driver to circumnavigate round the block a little while you get ready perhaps?'

Her criticism of my crumpled trousers and muddy hands hung unspoken in the morning air. 'Not at all, Mrs Chatergee. It won't take a moment for me to wash my hands, and real linen always creases, don't you find?'

All was well, and we had started on our mutually enjoyable exchange of put-downs, officially known as English lessons. Mrs Chatergee's husband owned the Udaipur Uretha Factory which made them wealthy. It had not, in Mrs Chatergee's opinion, however, given her the social standing to which she felt entitled. We had met at a grim British Council function where she'd suggested that we could be, mutually beneficial to each other; I would give her lessons on English culture and she would reciprocate with Indian. 'Although of course, Mrs Firth, I consider myself Rajashthani first, rather than just Indian. Descended from the Moguls, you know.'

It had taken a deal of courage to suggest to Mrs Chatergee that money would be far more acceptable to me, and she was naturally delighted.

'Of course, Mrs Firth, I do understand, and naturally it will be our little secret, though of course I am a little surprised. I had thought Dr Firth to be a University Man.'

Dr Firth? Where had that sprung from? 'Indeed so, Mrs Chatergee, but he has sacrificed his academic career in order to concentrate on his book. The money is unimportant.'

'Oh certainly, certainly, it must be such a privilege looking after a great literary man.'

Well, perhaps if I was, I thought sardonically, recalling the empty whisky bottles and dirty socks strewn round our bedroom.

'You will, of course,' she went on, 'have been to our beautiful Lake Palace Hotel for dinner?'

We had only been to their *Eat as Much as You Like for 150 Rupees* buffet after we'd first arrived, and it was certainly a most beautiful palace, set on an island on Lake Pichola. But because of our lack of money, any further meals out had been at Kwality Restaurant on Station Road. Cheaper still, was Ravi's, where he liked to place us in full view in the window to encourage the tourists.

I'd replied instead, 'We did enjoy our dinner there, but Dr Firth finds that it aids his digestion to eat more simply. Compared to that, the surroundings are unimportant.'

'Oh I do sympathize, digestion is so very important. But, Mrs Firth, is it not compared *with*? Please forgive if this is not so.'

I seated her firmly on the verandah, and blessed the rambling bougainvillea and hibiscus, which not only gave it shade, but also held the rotting timbers together. There would be no need this morning to take her into the house, and I could quickly make tea we could drink outside. The punkah fan had broken and Roland hopefully would not appear until after lunch. But you never knew. It depended largely on the quantity of Black Monk he'd drunk the previous evening, and he could be a little erratic. I did nag him about drinking local whisky in the heat because of his high blood pressure, but he told me it was now his one true pleasure. As I, obviously, was not. But I did, foolishly still love him.

Undoubted lech though he was, Roland Firth was a very attractive man when I first met him. Added to that, he had all the attributes I had been looking for. Having failed the Eleven Plus, I had later deliberately sought out men who would prove that I was not stupid. There had been evenings spent with pedantic teachers, evenings with poets, and one awful evening with a man who said he was writing a novel and needed research for the Sex Interest. Many classes and a young husband later, at a Poly I met Roland.

And here I was on a hillside in Udaipur with an elderly man to whom I am not married, no money, except a small pension, and a family that has almost given up on me. While the kettle was boiling, I read my elder sister Pamela's last letter. She was, as always, anxious to put me in the picture with everything I had left behind.

Dear Jane

Hope you are well. Chance meeting with your Alan in Abingdon Sainsbury's today. He looks rather sad and was buying Chicken Korma For One - and lots of other very unsuitable foods. He's obviously not hooked up with anyone else, which surprises me since he is now Manager of Jackson's Shoe Department and is driving a really nice little Vauxhall Vectra. Looked new but didn't see it properly as he drove off quite fast.

How is your job at the British Council going? (I had stretched my English conversations with Mrs Chattergee a little for effect.) *I expect you meet all sorts of interesting colonial people there - we saw* Jewel in the Crown *again on the tele last week - you know the film about this nice young English girl from a good family who goes with an Indian? I did think that at least your Ronald is English. Has he finished that book yet? Let us know and I'll look out for it at WH Smiths - or really he should send us a signed copy.*

I did not think that the book buyers of WH Smith would be so barmy as to invest in *Civilization and the Myths of Humanity*, even when, or more likely if, it ever got finished.

Anyway, no hope of you coming back I suppose? We do wish you'd write a bit more often. I'm not sure even if you've got married to Ronald?

If you did, was it with lots of flowers round your neck and chanting? We get a bit confused with what we see on the tele.
   With lots of love,
   Pamela
PS   I've got Alan's address if you ever wanted to write.

Exasperating and predictable though my sister could be, the letter made me homesick, even though she'd got his name wrong. And no, I did not want to write to Alan. That part of my life was now history.

I made the tea and covering the tin tray with an embroidered linen cloth, took it out to the veranda. I wanted to get back to Mrs Chattergee before she could go on the prowl, and discover the true frugality of our existence. But before we'd agreed on the exact protocol of calling cards, Roland appeared. He was unshaven and unsteady on his feet. His dressing-gown flapped open at the front. His shaking hand held a glass from which slopped some dark liquid. And he was very, very angry.

'Bloody Hell, woman, what you doing with visitors - can't you see I'm workin'?'

No, in very truth, I could not see that. The fact that *I* was, and bringing in some small income, was lost on him. He lurched a little and fixed Mrs Chatergee with a Stare.

'You come for the cleaning job? We'll need references - and I like it quiet in the mornings so I can get on with my book. No banging the pots in the kitchen, eh, there's a good girl.'

Mrs Chattergee spilt some tea down the impeccable navy suit and rose to her feet. 'Please call my Chauffeur,' she managed, 'I think we are all done here.'

Roland had blundered away, and later I heard a crash at the back of the house. I was so angry, I did not go to investigate.

*

The turnout at the tiny British cemetery was surprisingly good, especially since Roland had offended most of our few acquaintances. I recognized James Drayton from the British Council Library, and the two elderly Mayling sisters with whom Roland had loved to flirt.

Almighty God, we commend the soul of our brother, Roland ...

I was jerked back to what was happening at the graveside. The sun now shone directly overhead and bounced off the cheap brass handles of the coffin. I felt sorry for the grave-digger who had had to hack away at the baked earth to make the hole.

Earth to earth, ashes to ashes, dust to dust ...

I knew clearly then what I wanted to do. I wanted to go *round* the Earth, not *into* it. I reached down to the bag by my side, and drew out the manuscript of *Civilization and the Myths of Humanity*. The mourners were patient as, page by page, I floated them down onto the coffin. A slight breeze came from nowhere, and they eddied and fluttered into the grave.

It was very quiet and very hot.

Prakash came silently up to stand beside me. Together we looked down at the little lettuces, now turning yellow - either through too much watering or too much sun - or perhaps too much love? No, I decided, there could never be too much love.

'I think Madam, that they are now died. They not meant for here.'

And neither was I.

We smiled at each other and solemnly shook hands. I understood him perfectly.

'Beetroots will be better,' he said.

Eileen

A Family Affair

Peter leans on the fence which separates the woods from the farmland. In the distance the cows are grazing in the meadow and, in the field between, young Mark is driving the tractor cutting the grass, up and down he goes. Farther down in an old barn, now used for timber, the sound of the saw can be heard and men, methodically stacking the wood outside, add purpose to the idyllic scene. A few yards from the barn is the two hundred year old farmhouse, built in the traditional way, with winter shelter for the animals on the ground floor, hayloft above and above that living quarters, with the sleeping area under the eaves. Now used for storage for all manner of things, it has stood the test of time. A well-used road goes up the slope beside these buildings, leading past a group of much newer houses on either side, and disappears into a wooded area beyond.

Looking yet again at the letter in his hand, Peter sighs deeply, realising that the time has come for a major decision to be made. Turning to gaze up at the snow capped mountains, he draws strength from their peaks and feels somehow, deep within, that he must fight for just a little longer. Picking up his staff, he climbs steadfastly up the narrow path which will take him home to the modern, but still typically Swiss, farmhouse overlooking the land which has been in his family for generations and which he is now in danger of losing for ever.

That evening, Peter and the majority of the family sat around the large table, having enjoyed a good dinner, as they often did. Talking in turn as to what they thought should be done about the situation. Peter, his wife, Beatrice, his brother, Sven and wife, Verena, could no longer run the farm as they used to. Although they employed two young men to help them, and Mark, old Johan and his wife, Hannah, who were now too aged to do much, none of their offspring wanted to carry on with the family tradition of farming. Peter's son, Horst, worked for Mercedes Benz in Stuttgart and, married with two young children, did not want to return. His other son, Franz, also married with three young children, was a doctor in Zurich and his elder daughter, Petra, lived with her husband, Jacob, a plumber, and their two children in the nearby village. Her sister, Anita, was pursuing a career in the pharmaceutical industry in Geneva. Sven's sons, Lucca and Manfred, worked for banks in Zurich and daughter, Johanna, was married to Johan, an engineer.

The brothers had sold quite a lot of land surrounding the village years ago, rented the houses they had built, also years ago, and a cousin rented the lumberyard. Switzerland gave good subsidies to farmers, so the farm did well as did their little market shop in the village. The family name, Huber, was held in esteem for miles around and the village churchyard was filled with ancestors. As the patriarch, Peter, felt he and his brother, Sven, had worked so hard to keep this heritage for the future generations. It was devastating to have to sell to a conglomerate. They had tried to get people to manage the farm on a number of occasions but the cost of doing this was not viable. It would, in any case, create problems so, unless another buyer could be found quickly, the farm would have to be sold.

The brothers were willing to let the farm go at a very reasonable price to an individual buyer, rather than to the conglomerate, which was offering an indecently high price, but time was running out. A decision had to be made by the end of the month in nine days; otherwise the offer would be withdrawn.

Early next morning the telephone rang. Peter could hear Beatrice's cries of delight as she listened to whoever was on the line. After a few minutes, after replacing the receiver, Beatrice came into the dining room, grinning from ear to ear, and so excited she could hardly get the words out. She told Peter, Anita's, news. Anita would be bringing her fiancé to stay for a few days to discuss plans for their wedding. Peter gave his wife a bear hug and they both agreed it was wonderful news. Anita had pursued her career instead of paying attention to interested young men. Time had passed and everyone thought that Anita was wedded to her job.

For three days the future of the farm was forgotten whilst plans were made for a celebration. Anita and her fiancé arrived and once again the family were around the table. It turned out that Klaus farmed with his bothers in the Bernese Oberland and had met Anita when she made an excursion to Berne eighteen months ago. He had two young sons from a previous marriage and was delighted to be marrying a farmer's daughter who, he felt, would settle into the life knowing what it entailed.

Peter explained the dilemma that the family was in and asked Klaus, who would soon be a member of the family, to farm with them. Toasts were made to the agreement and next day the conglomerate was notified that the Huber farm would remain in their hands.

Leaving the bustle of the farmhouse, Peter called his dog, Max, and taking his staff, set off down the path to his favourite spot on the edge of the far wood where the deer often ventured out to nibble on the sweet grass. Leaning on the fence he could hear the cowbells ringing up on the high pasture. He waited patiently for the hawk to come and settle on the old stump near the original dwelling, as it did every evening. Now life was back to normal, the seasons will come and go as nature intended and the children, from our extended family, will grow and, in time, will hopefully take our place.

Elaine

A Tangled Web

'There's an answerphone message for you, Mum,' I called as I heard the front door slam.

'What's it about?'

'I think you'd better listen yourself.'

'Oh, all right. Why all the mystery?'

My mother came to the phone and pressed the 'play' button.

'Maureen, Donald's dead, ring me,' instructed a female voice.

'Oh dear, I'd better talk to her, I suppose.' With that Mum picked up the phone and dialled. 'Hallo Alice. I'm so sorry to hear your news.'

I left the room but heard my mother exclaim, 'Really? Is that a fact?' Then she said 'Well, I'll think about it,' and put the phone down.

Donald had been my mother's partner for a short while. As a teenager, I had resented his invasion of the cosy life Mum and I had built together after Dad died. So when he left Mum for her best friend, Alice, I wasn't sorry. Selfish of me, I know but I couldn't help my feelings. He wanted to be my special friend but I didn't want him for a dad or a friend. Mum tried to hide her hurt but she was depressed for a long time and deeply upset when, after living together for two years, he and Alice married.

Mum and Alice had been friends from school days. The two women were very different; Mum was big boned with a true Irish complexion and dark hair, though it needed a little help these days; in contrast, Alice was fair and petite. Mum had stood by Alice when, aged 14, she'd became pregnant.

'Bringing such disgrace to your family. How could you?' The head teacher had asked. However, after the baby girl was born and had been adopted, Alice was allowed to return to school. She was very miserable and quiet. Mum was sure she'd have kept the baby had Alice's parents agreed but that was not to be. Sadly, she'd had no more children.

I was curious to find out what Alice had asked Mum to do but had to be patient till the next day. It was Monday. Mum phoned me at work and asked me to meet her for lunch.

'But I'll see you this evening,' I protested. I'd arranged to have lunch with Alan and was looking forward to that.

'Please, Beth. It is important.'

'Oh! OK, Mum. I'll meet you in The Rose and Crown at one o'clock.'

'Thanks, Angel,' she replied. This must be serious, I thought. She only calls me 'Angel' on the rare occasions she wants my help or advice. She's very independent most of the time.

Alan said we could make lunch another day but he didn't sound too pleased.

The Rose and Crown was only five minutes from my office and Mum was at the bar when I got there.

'What do you want to drink?' she asked

'Just an apple juice, please,' I replied, glancing up at the blackboard menu. 'What's the soup today?'

'Stilton and broccoli,' answered the barmaid, pulling a pint to serve the man beside me.

'Yes, please, with brown bread but no butter.'

'Same for me,' added my Mum.

We moved to a table by the window, drinks in hand.

'Now, Mum, what's up?'

'Let me sit down, Beth, and I'll tell you.' She sank into the saggy armchair with a sigh of relief and took a sip from her glass. 'Now,' she began, 'Alice has asked me to help her write a eulogy for Donald. What do you think?'

'Bloody cheek, frankly, Mum! After all, she stole him from you.'

'Oh Beth! She did me a favour really. Made me see what an idiot I'd been falling for him in the first place. But I could tell her a thing or two that'd make her eyes boggle!'

'Like what?'

Our soup arrived, steaming and inviting.

What she told me shook me. Startled I took a gulp of the hot soup and burnt my tongue, 'But Mum,' I protested, 'you can't put such things in a eulogy.'

'Maybe not, but it'll be fun trying!' laughed my mother.

Heavens, what next, I thought

Donald's story was anything but straightforward. As a salesman, he'd travelled throughout the country, sometimes staying away from home for weeks at the time. He had the 'gift of the gab' and was good at his job. A charming man, but his intention to grow old disgracefully had been cut short when he died aged fifty-eight. He was adored by the ladies, each of whom thought she was the one for him. Jane, his first wife and eleven years his senior, had thrown him out, tired of the endless string of mistresses. Apparently, they'd had a joint-holiday home in Florida and after things went wrong, they'd flown out on the same plane to arrange its sale. In Miami, Donald hired a car and, leaving Jane at the airport, drove to the apartment and stayed there for almost four months, entertaining all the girls he could find. No wonder she divorced him.

'What happened to Jane? I asked.

'I don't really know,' Mum replied, 'but I think she died a few years ago.'

'She's got him back then,' I laughed.

'You're wicked, Beth. Well,' she continued, 'I think I'll agree to Alice's request. Get her to put a notice in a national paper announcing the funeral, then sit back to see who turns up.'

'Doesn't Alice know what sort of man he was? Perhaps she won't be surprised.' I insisted.

'She's so naïve,' laughed Mum, 'totally blinded by this darling little boy who never grew up. He was great fun to be with,' she added ruefully.

'What are you going to do, Mum?'

'I'll go and see her. Test the water.' She replied mischievously, 'See you tonight and thanks for listening.'

Back in the office, it was hard to concentrate. I found the whole situation very funny and imagined the grave scene with Donald's women of various ages weeping and throwing flowers onto his coffin.

A few days later an announcement appeared in *The Daily Telegraph:*

Pearson – Donald George 14 Feb 1950-21 June 2008. Beloved husband of Alice, died suddenly on Saturday. Small family cremation on Monday, 30th June. Family flowers only. Donations, if desired, for the Nell Gwynne Charitable Trust, can be sent to Tony's Funeral Services, 24 The High, Alterton. A Service of Thanksgiving for his Life to be held on 5th September 2008, 1.30pm at St Mary's Church, Olverton and afterwards at Olverton Village Hall. Kindly indicate attendance to Maureen Bartlett on 01... or Maureen@mbartlett.net.

Pity, I thought, no chance of any weeping and flower throwing at the graveside.

So the scene was set. Alice agreed with Mum that this was the best arrangement. The minister willingly undertook to say a few words about Donald at the crematorium, leaving Alice to sort out a eulogy for the thanksgiving service in September. I went to keep Mum company at the funeral, which was just as well as few people came. Donald's brother and family, and Alice's two spinster sisters turned up. The minister did his best and spoke of Donald as a hard working and caring husband despite his work taking him away from home so much. He droned on for some time and I must have drifted off.

During July and August the phone seemed to be ringing day and night, though some callers left strange messages and we weren't sure about one or two of the emails. Could they be spam? The list of those wishing to attend the thanksgiving service grew. Alice was amazed by the number of women who'd known Donald. Mum pointed out that some of the B&Bs he stayed at would have been owned by spinsters or widows. But even she was taken by surprise when someone called Gladys phoned declaring she was Donald's wife and had been for 6 years. I picked up the extension and listened. When pressed, she admitted she'd declined his offer of marriage. 'Don't believe in it,' she'd said but she'd changed her name to his by deed poll for the sake of their two children. She declared she didn't know about Alice and screamed at my mother as if she was in some way to blame. Gladys insisted that she and their children should have been at the funeral. Donald was their father after all. They would definitely come to the thanksgiving service. Mum was very upset and I interrupted:

'Hallo! I'm Beth, Maureen's daughter. How old are the children?' I demanded

'Three and four,' said Gladys meekly.

'Don't you think they're too young?'

'Maybe you're right. But how will I cope without him,' she wailed, 'What do I tell his babies?'

A candidate for the *Nell Gwynne Charitable Trust*, I thought. 'She can't be much older than me, Mum.'

'Well, no, probably not. It's odd, but she sounds strangely familiar. Poor Alice. What shall I tell her?'

'Keep shtum for the moment, Mum. Maybe Gladys won't come.'

'Oh dear! Why ever did I agree to be the contact?'

'How are you and Alice getting on the eulogy?'

'Slowly's not the word for it! I'm spending this weekend with her to really work on it. The thanksgiving service is only 10 days away.'

Good, I thought, Alan and I can have the house to ourselves for two whole days at long last.

September came all too quickly. Gladys hadn't been in touch again but I wasn't very optimistic about the good lady staying away. I couldn't get it out of my mind what Mum had said '... she sounds strangely familiar...'

Alice and Mum greeted everyone as they arrived at the church. It was obvious which people they knew, Donald's work colleagues and family members, but there were a few awkward moments when women neither of them knew introduced themselves. As the opening hymn was ending, the door opened and a neatly dressed fair-haired woman with two young children came into the dimly lit church. They were ushered into a pew at the back and my heart sank. O Lord, this must be Gladys.

In a blur the service continued and then it was time for the eulogy. After a great deal of debate, Mum had been persuaded to read it and she made her way up the aisle and turned to face the congregation.

'Thank you for joining Alice this afternoon to celebrate Donald's life. It is good to see so many of his friends. Many more have been in touch with messages of condolence and warmth; messages which have astonished his wife by the depth of affection and love with which he was regarded. Donald enjoyed a varied life, travelling the country for his job, sharing his knowledge, expertise and friendship with very many people. His work colleagues have told tales of his ability as a salesman and Alice is grateful for the way he was looked after in the B&Bs where he stayed on his numerous trips.' I kept my eyes on the floor not daring to look at the ladies in the congregation. Mum continued extolling the virtues of this Lothario, ending with: 'Donald was a fun-loving, hard-working and caring man, loved by everyone who knew him. We will all miss the warmth and support of a very dear and close friend.'

During the final hymn I made my way to the back of the church and quietly introduced myself to the late arrival. Yes, it was Gladys, about thirty-five, I thought. But where had I seen her before? I explained Mum and I hadn't told Alice of her existence.

'Is that Alice?' she asked, pointing to the front pew. I nodded. At that moment, Alice turned, and the penny dropped.

Wasn't I sitting beside a younger version of Alice?

Eve

65

Gelid World

Witnessed only by the billions of stars in the galaxy, an explosion of opposing gases rippled shock waves across time and tilted a minor sun a few degrees and Earth's weather was changed forever.

* * *

The Blue Sun rose like an iced diamond in the northern sky. Its cold light fell on a stream. Silver fishes flashed between green fronds and danced with the current. Gradually everything slowed. Changed from a watery paradise to frozen glass.

Birds took flight, seeking shelter in hollows, eaves or barns. Grasses, autumn foliage and the brown bark of the trees – whitened.

A farm lay as if in death. No creature could be seen and the shapes of barns and fences were like artists' outlines. In the lowland, fields no longer ripened with the seasons. They were enclosed under artificial screens that were stiffening in the northerly breeze.

Painted on this whiteness, the farmhouse smoke swirled from the chimney and its windows were shuttered. The grey brick was coated with a clear film, its purpose to trap the heat within. But nothing could stop the ice covering the house.

A frozen world locked in a time capsule for the next ten days.

Shelly Collins groped for the alarm stopper; then slid her dark head back under the duvet. She ran her hand over the empty half of the bed, missing Rick's strong warm body. His promotion was great. She just didn't like him being away at Control HQ.

Images of recent years came to mind. The twenty-first century may have come in with flamboyant celebrations, but had drowned in worldwide mayhem twenty years later. Shelly had lived through a world catastrophe. Technology was useless. Ten out of every ninety days the Blue Sun dominated the world's weather.

Nowhere on the planet did the Yellow Sun's warmth exist.

Throwing back the cover she groaned, 'Staying tucked up warm and snug isn't getting today's work done.'

Stripes, the ginger cat, stretched in his basket when Shelly went into the kitchen.

'Hi, lazy bones, breakfast?'

Both fed and satisfied, Shelly pulled on her Ranger thermal jump-suit, rider clothes and crash helmet.

'Bye, ginger, see you tonight.'

Then she went out, locking the door of Bayford Lodge - now known as Freeze Station Alpha 7.

Ten minutes later, the snow-scooter was a red slash across the white face of the hillside. Far below, in the valley, a wide meandering river had become a slippery grey snake. The muted colours of the weeds would disappear as the ice thickened in the days to come.

Shelly made several calls to remote farms and by mid-afternoon she reached Primrose Cottage, which looked as though a fairy had put a spell on it. Hanging from the roof, drips of rain had turned into glass needles and creeping ice made the leaded windows look cracked. Crimson, yellow and bronze dahlias were taking on white coats.

In answer to her knock, she heard feet shuffling down the corridor. Several bolts slid back and Dora Cottrell's wrinkled face peeped through a crack. Pale blue eyes brightened and the door swung open.

'Sergeant Collins. Come in, my girl.'

Taking off her helmet Shelly brushed flaked ice from her jacket.

'New uniform?' Dora asked, as Shelly sat down at the kitchen table.

'Yes. Improved insulation, for the days when I'm out and about in these sub-zero temperatures. New badge too: Freeze Ranger.'

Dora placed a steaming mug of coffee in front of Shelly and then settled into a chair.

'I like the red colour, matches your snow-scooter. Very fashionable.'

'Thanks.'

'How are things in the big wide world?'

'Fair to middling. I would never have wished this upon us, but it has brought about a global union. That would never have happened otherwise.' Shelly sipped her coffee. 'There's talk of a Global Committee. Who knows, it may work?'

'Pigs might fly and elephants born pink, but I'll keep my fingers crossed.' Dora pulled a thick woollen cardigan from a stool and put it on. 'The temperature's starting to go down.'

When Shelly left Dora's the afternoon light was fading.

She rode into Maddock Valley and felt dwarfed by the high cliffs that stood like white marble walls, the grey crevices dark windows. Nearer the valley floor smaller rocks resembled steps. The air temperature was colder here and snowflakes started to fall. Then the wind strengthened and it turned into a blinding snowstorm. The single-track road became a ribbon of ice. The rear of the scooter was set up as a half-track, but this didn't stop the front wheels skidding and although Shelly fought the slide, it veered into the scree. Body and machine parted company.

Shelly fell onto the rocks. Jagged points pierced her side and shoulder. Her helmet smashed against the rear track as the scooter flew past her on a collision course with the ground.

She lay motionless, senses stunned; it was the searing pain that kept her conscious.

As she moved, a cry left her lips, 'Bloody hell! Think! Breathe slowly … phone … scooter.' She found voicing her needs helped control the pain. 'It's getting dark … shelter.' Rolling onto her uninjured side, Shelly pulled herself up against a boulder. Her legs worked and one arm. But her left side felt on fire.

The snow-scooter had ended up on its side. It looked OK, but looks could be deceiving.

Five minutes later, Shelly knew she was in trouble.

The petrol tank had fractured and the snow was soaking up the life-saving liquid.

Her Global Tracking System was in her left inside pocket, but she knew, before her fingers lifted it out, that it was broken.

She now had three priorities – shelter, warmth and help.

Her last report into Area 7 HQ had indicated that she was on her homeward run.

On an impulse, she had turned off into Maddock Pass to call on Harry Stubbs. He had fallen and broken his pelvis during the Summer Freeze Time. Orders emphasised that straying from the reported route was dangerous.

It was almost dark and the snowstorm had worsened. Flakes built in layers on her uniform and the cold was biting through into her flesh. She needed to find shelter, *now!* Taking the survival backpack from the scooter she found the weight was unbearable on her shoulder. She would have to carry it round her waist.

The howling wind and snow forced her to bend almost double to shield her visor and each step could cause her to slip and maybe break an ankle. If she fell she wouldn't be able to get up. Pain spread from her shoulder across her chest, making it difficult to breath. 'How much further?' she shouted. Then the cliff face towered out of the storm.

Shelly ran her gloved fingers along the white surface wanting to kiss the cold stone and, under the lee of the cliff, the wind was less fierce. She started to search for a crevice large enough for her, and the sleeping bag she needed to survive the night. Relief surged as she felt an opening. Bitter disappointment as her fingers penetrated just a few inches.

Her eyes flooded with tears and she blinked several times to stop them rolling down her face. The cold and pain were sapping her strength and Shelly dug deep into her mental reserves to carry on along the cliff.

Minutes seemed like hours. Then Shelly felt the opening to a cave – it was big enough for her to get in. Huddled on the ground and with her good hand she pulled the sleeping bag into shape and crawled between the warm fibres. There was a dent in her helmet, but it would be unwise to take it off. If there were a cut and blood underneath, it would have to soak into her short curls. The insulation began to warm her and she closed her eyes, then they snapped open. 'You mustn't go to sleep.' She repeated this over and over as the hours ticked by to the dawn.

Rick Collins flipped his mobile off. He looked at his watch for the tenth time in the last half-hour. Where the hell was Shelly? His wife might be the most independent, I-can-look-after-myself woman, but it was almost midnight. This was the first day of Freeze Time. There should be no emergencies yet.

Rick went into the Control HQ Ops Room and Sergeant Wilkins turned from the display screen. 'Bob, I need to contact Shelly's control unit. Can I use your set?'

'Be my guest. Trouble?'

'There's no reply from home. I need to know what's going on.'

Rick sat down and dialled up Area 7. After a few minutes his face tightened and he asked, 'You received no sign-off call? It's gone midnight, George. Something has happened.'

Bob Wilkins listened to the one sided conversation: Shelly was missing … no SOS received … unable to search until daylight.

'You'll let me know the minute you hear from her? Thanks.' Rick ended the transmission.

Bob spoke, 'Shelly's a bright girl; she would have got in touch if anything was wrong.'

Rick sat silent. His mind wouldn't work. He couldn't think what to do, where to go. All he could picture were mountains covered in ice, roads and tracks deadly skid pans and a red snow-scooter scattered in pieces. Shelly lying injured, maybe dead.

In the cave, Shelly watched the dark turn to dawn.

Now was the time to switch on her Personal Locator Beacon, but she needed to be outside for the rescue satellite to pick up her signal.

The minute she moved every muscle in her body exploded with pain. Beads of perspiration soaked her forehead and body heat misted her visor. She was suffocating. Wrenching the facemask up, she breathed in ice cold air. This took her breath away and another searing pain shot across her chest. Shelly controlled her panic by inhaling slowly.

Standing was impossible. Her left side had stiffened, preventing any movement, so she crawled, using her other side. Reaching the cave entrance, the Blue Sun mocked her as it rose for the second morning to increase the cold temperature on Earth.

Hanging the beacon round her neck, Shelly activated the signal. The sleepless hours caught up with her and her head dropped forward and she dozed.

Shelly woke when the first pebble hit her helmet, then a stone, then several, then a bombardment of rock crashed down around her. She screamed, 'No! Not now!' She dragged her injured body back into the cave and watched with horror as the opening was blocked with falling rocks.

Groping in the darkness, she found her survival pack, then the torch. The roof sloped from the opening down to nothing. A wedge of stone pitted with holes, like Gruyere cheese. The simile reminded her she was hungry. The pack had emergency food, water and a small stove. She needed a hot drink. Lighting the stove proved difficult one-handed, but she managed to make hot soup.

Zipped back in the sleeping bag, Shelly tried to be positive and talked to herself. It seemed to focus her mind:

'Yes, I was outside long enough for my signal to be received by HQ. They will find my scooter - know I can't be far away.'

Time passed. How long she didn't know, her watch was broken.

Ice began to whiten her sleeping bag. Coolness crept over her skin and puffs of mist left her mouth as she breathed out. She had felt panic yesterday outside in the valley, now, trapped behind the rock fall, this cave could be her tomb.

'Rick, come for me, *please*. Don't leave me here to die.'

*

At Control HQ, rescue boss Tom Shepherd, was prepared and ready to leave as soon as it was light. He was a big, muscular man, with white wavy hair, in his mid fifties. He had climbed and walked the mountain ranges since a boy. All he needed for a quick and successful retrieval was Shelly's signal.

'We've got her on satellite,' Bob shouted from the Ops Room.

Hearing the shout, Rick looked up from the rucksack he was packing.

They had her. Thank God.

He waited for the co-ordinates to be marked on the map.

An hour later, two rescue vehicles entered Maddock Pass.

A leaden sky blocked out the Blue Sun and the dull whiteness of the valley sent a shudder down Rick's spine. Conditions were bad, considering it was only the second freeze day.

'Maybe we should have used a helicopter, Tom.'

'Yeh, progress is slow, but we're nearly there, another couple of miles.'

The red snow-scooter was hard to spot after the snowstorm. Even the shape had taken on a rock formation.

'Stop! Over there, on its side, her scooter.'

Rick was out of the cabin before the snowmobile came to a halt.

Red-suited Rangers fanned out across the frozen rocks, searching to and fro, like worker ants. Shelly was nowhere to be found.

Tom called HQ. 'Can you re-affirm the co-ordinates? Over.'

'Signal ceased. Has not restarted. Over.'

Rick snatched the handset. 'You *must have it*, those batteries last over twenty-four hours.'

Tom took the handset back. 'Rick, calm down, there must be a reason for the signal to stop. Call the team back for a new briefing.'

Beyond the circle of torchlight, the cavern walls oozed coldness from their stone pores.

Shelly's breathing became laboured as the oxygen decreased. She fought the urge to close her eyes, knowing if she did, it would be her final sleep.

Since the rock fall there had been scuttling noises and her four-legged companion ran up her sleeping bag. 'How are you, Ratty? Warmer than me I'm sure.' A nose and whiskers explored her visor; then it settled between her feet.

Into the silence came a faint scraping sound, growing louder with each precious breath.

Was it rescue or another rock fall?

Shelly closed her eyes. She knew if it was not rescue, her life was ended.

Outside, Rick heaved away the rocks. They were still grey, which meant the fall had been recent. He wouldn't let his mind accept that Shelly was crushed under them.

'Tom, an opening, there *is* a cave.'

Rick frantically strained at the heavy rocks, but he made an opening. His gloves ripped through to the flesh.

He crawled in and stopped. A yellow glow picked out the still body.

He cried out, *'No! We're too late!'*

He lifted her shoulders and a groan passed her lips, then she opened her eyes and looked at him.

'I knew you would come for me.' With these words Shelly slipped into unconsciousness.

*

Later that day, Rick marched along the hospital corridor, chocolates in one hand and flowers in the other. He had his speech prepared – reckless, stupid, dangerous behaviour. It was time she gave up policing and started pushing a pram.

All this flew out the window, when Rick saw Shelly's white face and dark bruises, her beautiful eyes covered by closed lids

'Hi sweetheart, are you awake?' Rick kissed her forehead.

'No.'

'Then open up. See what I have for you.'

'I can't. I feel a fool.' Keeping her eyes closed, she continued, 'I love you. I was wrong and I'm sorry, but I'm not giving up being a Ranger.'

She opened her eyes and looked at him.

'Fine by me. A lesson learned, my love.'

How come she could always twist him round her little finger?

What the hell, pram pushing could wait another year.

Julie

Gone to Earth

Evelyn walked into my failing bookshop on a bright April morning. I recognised her immediately. Her photograph had been in the local paper; she'd bought the manor house a few miles away from our small market town, intending to create another garden. The article said she'd made important gardens in her previous two homes with her late husband and was a leading light of the Royal Horticultural Society.

Yawn, yawn, I thought, when I read it - can't stand gardening. In the flesh she looked a jolly lady, about forty, ten years older than me.

I greeted her, 'Can I help you? Robert, at your service. We have a good gardening section.' I gave her my best smile, hoping she would spend some badly needed money.

She smiled warmly and I could see her eyes widen as she took in my height, build and chiselled features. Ah, I thought, she fancies me. This I learnt later was true - unfortunately she also fancied how much earth I could turn over with a spade!

'Wonderful,' she said. 'I take it you enjoy gardening?'

'One of my passions,' I lied. 'Unfortunately I can't indulge myself at the moment, I live above the shop.' I pointed to the ceiling. 'I'm afraid I've only got a window box.'

'Poor you,' she murmured sympathetically and bought three gardening books totalling over sixty pounds. Worth cultivating – ha, ha – I thought.

We married a year later. I swotted up on horticultural matters by reading all the gardening books in the shop and a few from the library. I enthused about whatever she was keen on: in January it was snowdrops – damned if I can tell a Merlin from a Magnet – they're all little white and green flowers to me - the price she paid for some bulbs was ridiculous. In March it was narcissi and the greatest bore of all came in June with the old roses and the fucking clematis! Dreadful twining plants, always catching wilt or some other disease. I hated it when she made me spray them with some revolting fungicide.

There were many compensations: I lived a comfortable life, no money worries – I gave up the bookshop after we'd been married a year. The fly in the ointment was that she insisted on a premarital settlement – I wouldn't get a penny if we divorced, but I'd be quids in if she died, and she *was* older than me. Hope springs eternal!

I had to work in the garden, which I hated, but worse, I had to put up with Jasper, her faithful basset-hound. I hated that dog and the feeling was mutual. Jasper was five years old when we married.

At the beginning I tried to make friends with him, though dogs and cats are not my thing.

'Good boy,' I shouted, throwing his blue-rubber ball, which made metallic noises as it bounced over the grass, but he curled his upper lip disdainfully and stalked away from me towards Evelyn, tail up, his red-eyed anus glaring at me.

'He's jealous, darling,' she cooed and showered kisses on his saliva-drenched face. Disgusting!

'Who's got a lovely coat?' she cried, 'My darling boy has!'

I presumed she wasn't talking about me.

After five years of Jasper, I'd had enough. He was older, smellier and dribbled all over me - on purpose. Whenever Evelyn was out I opened the gates and encouraged him to wander down the road. I persevered and bingo! At the third attempt he was run over.

'Robert, how could you be so careless to leave the gate open. Poor Jasper! My darling boy,' she sobbed.

'Not guilty, Evelyn,' I said. 'It must have been the postman.' I *found* a hole in the hedge, which I'd made previously, and showed it to her. She nodded sadly, her suspicions allayed.

'I was fond of the old boy too,' I said.

'I know you were, dear. You can bury him at the top of the garden – it was his favourite view.'

I enjoyed digging that hole and planting him in it. I pretended to be upset and muttered suitable words of mourning as she cast rose petals into his grave and sobbed. Silly bitch!

I planted a St Edmund's Pippin apple over him in the autumn. It'll be well manured, I thought, grinning as I pictured Jasper rotting in the earth. I planted montbretias around the base of the tree, mainly because Evelyn dislikes them – she regards them as a common weed.

The one-year sapling has grown into a productive tree and I enjoy coming to this part of the garden, sitting on the nearby bench and biting into one of the apples – they ripen in early September.

'One in the eye for you, Jasper,' I mutter every year, as I chew into the firm and juicy flesh.

On my fifty-second birthday I walked up the garden feeling frustrated and depressed. Evelyn had gone to a Royal Horticultural Show in London with the Thompsons. She couldn't be bothered celebrating my birthday. I was glad to see the back of her: she was driving me mad with her continual nagging about drinking too much and how I should see the doctor about an anger-management course.

I walked past the formal flower beds - how I hate their contrived blending of colours; past the Japanese garden with its pretentious red lacquer bridge. On through the orchard to the wilder part of the garden, which ends with a view over the valley.

I sat on the bench near the St. Edmund's Pippin. I can't stand this life much longer, I thought. I still had my good looks. Thank God they'd ceased to interest her several years ago. The menopause had slowed down her considerable sex-drive. The sight of her bulging body and hands coarsened by continually scrabbling in the soil, had made having sex with her a sickening chore. At the dreaded call: 'Shall we have an early night, Robert?'

I was only able to do my duty by closing my eyes and imagining I was making love to Claudia Schiffer, Angelina Jolie or some other nubile female I had seen in a newspaper or film.

Oh, to be able to make love to someone like Sophie, the barmaid at the Horse and Jockey; slim with pert, small breasts. The only compensation for pumping away for England had been a present or a cheque the next day. I was dependent upon her - I should have got a regular allowance sorted out with a solicitor when we married.

I slumped on the bench. It was a perfect June day: no air movement, the temperature about seventy-five as the sun approached its zenith. There was no noise - the birds had deserted this part of the garden. Despite the warmth of the day I suddenly felt a chill around my legs, as though a miasma of dank air was coiling round my ankles. I lent down and rubbed them. Was I developing rheumatism?

I looked at the St Edmund's Pippin. The crop looked promising, the tiny apples swelling, though the dreaded June drop had not started. I grinned as I thought of Jasper lying there - nothing but bones by now.

All the leaves of the tree were still, but a movement at its base caught my eye. One of the sword-like leaves of the montbretia was waving with a regular rhythm. I watched it fascinated: back and forth it moved, like the hand of a metronome. Only this one leaf moved. Was something shaking it? A mouse, perhaps? I moved closer to see if I could find the creature and as I did, the movement of the leaf became faster. Suddenly I realised what it reminded me of: it was like a wagging dog's tail, and its momentum increased as I came closer - as though it was welcoming me - as though it knew who I was.

A cold sweat came over me. I backed to the seat and sat down, my gaze never leaving the moving leaf. As I retreated the waving slowed, but it kept up its deliberate beat. My body was icy cold, yet beads of sweat ran down my face. My heart was racing and I felt I was losing consciousness. I closed my eyes and tried to take some deep breaths.

I began to feel calmer. Warmth came back into my body and I was relieved when I heard birds singing. I felt a breeze against my cheek and when I opened my eyes all the leaves of the tree and those of the montbretias were dancing.

I got up and stiff-legged made my way back to the house, cursing myself for a fool and letting my imagination run riot. A dog's tail indeed! It was Evelyn - she was getting on my nerves. She was making me ill. I'd got rid of Jasper – now it was Evelyn's turn.

That evening I went to the Horse and Jockey for dinner and when I got home I poured myself a large whisky and settled down in the sitting room to watch Prime Suspect 12. If only someone would murder Evelyn. Perhaps a maniac would attack her on the train. I smiled as I imagined the police car coming to the house to break the sad news and how the young, attractive female constable would comfort me. When they'd gone I would dance around the house, open a bottle of champagne and start my life afresh.

I was grinning as I swallowed the last of my whisky and was on my way for a refill when the television went dead and the standard lamp went out. Bloody power cut, I thought.

The uncurtained French windows let in a pale light from the sickle moon, but the room had lost its colour. I heard a scratching noise outside the windows, as though there was an animal trying to get in. Then a baying. The same feelings of nausea, cold and fear that I had experienced that morning engulfed me again. I was frozen with terror.

From the direction of the window I heard a different noise coming towards me. A metallic chink, chink, chink, as something rolled across the carpet.

Suddenly the light came on, the television blared into life. I swear my heart nearly stopped. I looked down and there at my feet was a blue ball. Feelings of hatred and rage for Evelyn and the dead Jasper came over me. I saw the outline of an animal at the window, its eyes glaring, red in the reflected light.

I picked up the ball and hurled it at the window. It exploded into a thousand shards.

'Damn you to hell!' I shouted.

'Robert, what on earth is the matter? Are you ill?'

I turned.

Evelyn was standing in the doorway, behind her were the Thompsons.

'It's that bloody dog! He's haunting me!' I snarled.

Evelyn was as white as a sheet and the Thompsons looked shocked.

'What dog, dear?' Evelyn asked, as though talking to a child. She turned to Freddy Thompson, 'Ring for the doctor,' she hissed. 'Tell him Robert is not well.' She turned back to me. 'Now, Robert, sit down, dear. You say you've seen a dog?'

'Get your hands off me, you bitch. You've put him up to this. You've set Jasper on me!' I was furious.

'Jasper? Jasper is dead, Robert, surely you remember that?' Freddy returned and nodded to her. 'You see what I mean,' she said to him, 'he's not in control of himself. Please don't leave me alone with him.'

I pointed to the window, 'He's alive! He came to the window. He brought his ball for me!' I yelled.

Evelyn glanced at the Thompsons. 'Where is the ball, dear? I can't see a ball,' she said to me.

'I threw it at him. He'll come and get me – he'll kill me,' I shouted hysterically.

Evelyn clutched her hands to her throat, 'Now, Robert, calm down. We won't let him hurt you, will we?' She turned to the Thompsons for support. They shook their heads, their eyes popping out of their sockets.

I heard the sound of a car arriving and Freddy left the room and returned with the doctor. At last someone to help me! Freddy was speaking to him in a low voice. The doctor looked at me.

'Don't believe that swine,' I shouted, pointing to Freddy. 'You've got to get rid of Jasper! Get the police to dig him up and shoot the bastard!'

The doctor whispered to Evelyn and she nodded. The four of them moved towards me. The doctor had a syringe in his hand.

'He was waving his tail at me from the grave – he was outside the window.'

The doctor shook his head, 'Come along now. Sit down, roll up you sleeve. We'll soon make you better.

All fight left me and I collapsed onto the settee.

*

I woke up with a terrible thirst. I couldn't move. I opened my eyes and stared up at a white ceiling. One light shone from a recess. I tried to move my head, but it was painful. I was swathed in a white coat bound tight around me and was lying on a mattress on the floor. There was no one else in the room. I called out, but no one came.

Then I heard it. The panting of breath, regular and deep, was getting closer with each second. 'No! No!' I screamed. The same terrible feelings engulfed me again. I screwed my eyes tight, not wanting to see the phantom that was padding towards me. Then I felt the hot, humid breath on my cheek - smelling of the graveyard. I felt a rough, slimy tongue rasp my cheek. I screamed and hurtled into blackness.

My mistress visits me every week. She watches as I crawl round the floor and drink from my bowl. There is always someone with her.

She tentatively pats my head, 'His coat, I mean his hair, is still nice and shiny,' she says.

I love her. Why won't she take me home? I would be a good dog.

Vera

Air

Aquarius

THE BLACK AND BLUE CLUB

How does it feel to be born on St Valentine's Day?' asked Julie.

'I think I'm lucky; it's a lovely day for a birthday – so romantic,' replied Elaine, looking at her friends gathered round a table in The Unicorn.

'Aquarians can be unpredictable and rather detached, or so I've read,' said Eileen, cocking her head as though waiting for a confession.

Elaine pursed her lips. 'I have been given to understand that we seek new knowledge to break down old ideas. We are ahead of our time.'

'Elaine, you've been talking to Madame Belmondo again,' said Vera.

'Come on, Elaine, dish the dirt,' said Eve. 'Tell us a story about being unpredictable'.

Elaine sighed, 'Oh, all right, I know you won't stop teasing me until I do.

'I was nine years old, living in North Berwick and I was in love with Edward, a dark-haired, handsome boy of the same age. I thought he was wonderful and as our parents were friends we saw each other regularly.

"Would you like to join my club?" he asked.

Thrills! "Yes, please."

"You know the bridge near the stream?"

"Yes."

"Come there at three, this afternoon. I'll be waiting, underneath the bridge with the other members of the gang."

'I was so excited; I'd be a member of Edward's club. What did they do? I imagined we would romp through woods and fields, looking for birds' nests and picking wild flowers. Perhaps I could teach them to dance. Perhaps Edward would kiss me!

'That afternoon I hurried to the bridge. There were five children: Edward and two other boys and two girls, one holding her arm and crying.

"This is Elaine," Edward announced. "She's going to be initiated into the Black and Blue Club."

"Why is it called that, Edward," I asked.

'Edward pulled the crying girl forward. "Show her your arm, Susie."

'Susie sobbed and held out her arm. Just above the wrist were deep red marks.

'I didn't understand.

'"Tomorrow,' Edward proudly said, "the bruises will have turned black and blue. Hold out your arm, Elaine and I'll give you a Chinese burn!'

'He came towards me, a sadistic gleam in his eye.

'My arm came out, not to be tortured, but to thump him firmly on the chest. He fell down heavily and began to cry.

'"You horrid boy! I hope your bottom is black and blue tomorrow." I ran home before he had time to recover. Since then, I've never been a clubbable woman.'

Flight 3491

'Good morning, Maria. Please ask Guido to bring the car round in twenty minutes. Turning from the maid to her assistant, Alessandra adds, 'Now, Sofia, let me look at the fabrics you have brought me.'

'Yes, Madame Galotti, I have laid out the samples here on the table and I also have two swatches which are classics. Perhaps you could mix classics with the latest designs?'

'I will decide which fabrics to use, Sofia. Where are the trimmings and buttons? Alessandra walks over to the table. 'I intend to use many different buttons and add detachable large brooches made of wool, ribbon, petersham; perhaps even use some of the fabrics here.' She picks up a few pieces of material. 'My daughter has sent me a selection that she has made and I expect her to bring quite a number with her today.'

They continued their discussion until there is a knock at the door and Maria comes back into the room.

'The car is waiting, Madame. Will that be all?'

'Yes, Maria. Just remember to tell cook that we will have luncheon on the terrace and that there will be eight for dinner.'

'Yes, Madame.'

'Now, Sofia, I must go or I'm going to be late. The final sketches are in the blue portfolio on the desk. Please be kind enough to arrange them in sequence on the table and I'll attend to the final decision of what to use when I return. Oh! The brooches are in a box in the hall, if you'd sort them out as well? If Francesco calls, tell him I will call this evening. Ciao!'

*

Alessandra Galotti makes her way through the crowds in Arrivals and notes that the Flight 3491 from New York is delayed. A voice over the speaker system also gives this information. Irritated, Alessandra, widow turned fashion designer, makes her way towards the Executive Lounge. On entering, she pours herself a large cup of coffee and, taking a glass of orange juice from the table in front of her, walks swiftly to a corner table in the busy room.

Strange how things turned out; if Francesco and Claudia had not encouraged me to take up Fabio's suggestion to design some scarves for his collection three years ago, what would I be doing now? After Philippe's sudden fatal heart attack, more than four years ago, I was devastated - an absolute wreck. If it hadn't been for the children, I could easily have become a recluse or the exact opposite, a lost socialite going from one venue to another. Now I'm a designer for Fabio's famous couture house and lead a full and busy life.

Alessandra is brought out of her reverie by screams and shouts in the crowded lounge and then an eerie silence. Looking up she sees, on the television screen pictures of a burning aircraft. Fire fighters trying to put out the blaze, ambulance sirens blaring out and, in front of all that, a reporter repeating that behind him is Flight 3491, which took off for Leonardo Da Vinci, Rome but crashed landed at J F Kennedy, New York at the end of the runway. There are no survivors – no survivors. He gives a number to call. Shouting breaks out again in the lounge and there is a rush towards the door. Alessandra snatches her mobile from her bag. All she can think is that she must keep her emotions in check for now.

'Hello! Guido. Bring the car round to the entrance as quickly as you can. I have to get back to the Villa and find out what's happened.' My God! I hope there's been some mistake.

It can't be true that the plane's crashed and everyone's been killed.

Guido drives Alessandra home, both keeping their thoughts to themselves. On arrival at the security gates of the villa they are confronted by a number of reporters, but the police are there holding them back and allowing the car to pass through the gates. Sofia and Maria are waiting on the steps of the house.

'Have you seen or heard the news? What's happened? Tell me it's all a mistake; that it was another plane, not the one bringing Claudia and my grandchildren!'

They support her into the house.

'Come and sit down, Madame. Drink this, please. It will do you good.'

'Thank you, Maria. I must make some phone calls but I do feel faint. Perhaps if I just sit down for a few minutes, I'll feel better. Oh God, help me!' She buries her face in her hands.

'Salvatore wishes to speak with you, Madame Galotti.'

'Yes, yes, of course, Sofia. Send him in.'

The butler comes in looking distraught.

'Yes, Salvatore. You wish to speak with me?'

'Yes, Madame. It is with great sorrow that I must tell you that the news of the plane crash is true and it was Flight 3491 from New York to Rome.'

'Oh my God!' gasps Alessandra, wringing her hands.

'We are all shocked, Madame, continues Salvatore, 'but your son, Francesco phoned and is doing everything possible to acquire information. We are all so very very sorry. Shall I tell the reporters that you will give an interview tomorrow and hopefully that will satisfy them? Will you rest now, Madame? Maria can take you upstairs. There is nothing you can do at present.'

'Yes, Salvatore,' whispers Alessandra. 'Do whatever you think best.'

Alone at last in her room, Alessandra is able to give way to her emotions. Shaking and numb, she searches clumsily for the *Nembutal* in her bathroom cabinet, scattering its contents into the wash basin. In a daze she takes the tablets and without undressing, she slumps onto her bed, pulling the covers over her and weeps herself to sleep.

'Madame Galotti, wake up, wake up. Wonderful news; Claudia and the children were not on the plane. They are safe and on their way here now.'

Startled, Alessandra sits up, 'How can that be, Maria?'

'The flight was overbooked and so Claudia and the children came on another carrier which took off shortly before the original one. As it was diverted, she knew nothing about the crash until arriving here in Rome. Isn't it wonderful, Madame? Francesco will be here with them shortly.'

Alessandra shakes her head, disbelieving, 'I don't understand!'

'Your daughter phoned his office from the airport as soon as they landed.'

'Thank God! I have my family back again. Oh! Maria, I am so happy, so very, very happy.' She throws back the covers. 'I'll be down presently. It is indeed wonderful news.'

Looking through the window down on the well-kept gardens and lawns beyond, Alessandra feels calm and at peace with herself. Grateful for the circumstances which avoided a tragedy that would have had life changing consequences, not only for her, but for everyone concerned with the family. She realises that she must do something immediately.

For the relations, friends and colleagues of everyone on that doomed flight, their tragedy had just begun. The pain and suffering would be with them for the rest of their lives. Her thoughts turned to the anguish caused by so many needless deaths all over the globe. I must do something constructive to help people in distress, and not just financially, she decided. I have become a very selfish woman. There is so much I can contribute towards making a difference. Philippe would approve. Oh! My darling, how I miss you, but now I have a real purpose for my future.

Alessandra descends the staircase towards the sound of laughter and the excited voices of her family.

Elaine

Dance of the Flyers

Shirley looked at the large envelope. It had been sent by a gift company; but who from and what for? No time now, she'd overslept and was already late. She dropped it on the hall table and, shouting goodbye to Andrew, left for work. She cycled through the busy streets, fair hair streaming from beneath her helmet, wind on her face. Arriving at the office she quickly showered, changed and made her way to her office on the tenth floor.

'Hi, Mandy,' she called to her PA in the inner office.

Mandy looked up from her computer. 'Happy Birthday, Shirley,'

'Thank you,' she replied, 'What's on today? Any mail to deal with?'

Mandy joined Shirley and they spent the next couple of hours sorting the diary and clearing the in-tray.

'Doing anything special for your birthday?' asked Mandy picking up the documents for filing and turned to leave.

'No, but I've got a mystery present at home. I don't know who it's from or what it is.'

'You mean, you didn't open it before you left this morning?'

'No time. I was late for work as it was. Something to look forward to tonight though.'

'I couldn't have done that,' said Mandy. 'Curiosity would have got the better of me.'

To Shirley's surprise Andrew arrived to take her out to lunch. Things hadn't been good between them for some time. It was partly her fault, she knew. She shouldn't have made work an excuse for not going skiing with him over Easter. Unfortunately, he'd broken his leg but, when she picked him up at Gatwick, she was shocked to see Diane, his editor, among the passengers exiting Customs. They assured her they'd met by chance but of course they would say that, she thought. He worked from home and met Diane occasionally in her office but, with his leg in plaster, she'd come to see him once or twice. His third novel, about the Totonac Indians of Mexico, was due out in September and apparently they had a great deal to discuss.

'I see you haven't opened your gift yet,' he commented as he propped his crutches against the bar.

'No, I was late but I'll do it tonight. I wonder who sent it. How's the story going?'

'Well enough.' Andrew went on to tell her about the chapter he'd spent the morning on. It was the Totonac tale of a time of extreme drought, many centuries ago, when five young men decided they needed to implore Xipe Totec, God of Fertility, for the return of the rains. They found a tall straight tree in the forest and prayed to the tree's spirit to help them. Once they'd felled the tree, they carried it back to their village and, having stripped it of its branches, stood it in a hole.

To attract Xipe Totec's attention, four of them decorated themselves with feathers like birds, secured vines round their waists and also to the top of the pole. They 'flew' towards the ground whilst the fifth Indian played his flute and drum from the top of the pole. They pleaded to their God of Fertility.

'Sounds pretty dangerous,' remarked Shirley. 'Did it work?'

'It must have. Despite the Aztecs, there are still a good number of Totonac Indians in Mexico.' Andrew went on to explain how the four men paid homage from the top of the pole to the four corners of the earth, the four winds, the four elements and the four seasons. The vines were wound round the pole thirteen times, so when the men fell backwards, head-first, they spiralled thirteen times round the pole as they descended gracefully to earth. The total fifty-two rotations represented the number of years in the Totonac century.

'Do they still do it?'

'Yes, mostly for tourists. It's called *Danza de los Voladores.*'

'Oh, *Dance of the Flyers,* the title of your book. I'd love to see them do it,' said Shirley.

'Well, there's no reason why we couldn't go to Mexico, once I'm back on my feet; next year maybe. I love Mexico; spent some time there during my year out before university.'

Andrew had prepared supper by the time she got home. A glass of wine was waiting for her and beside it the envelope. Why was he being so considerate she wondered?

'The meal won't harm for a little while,' he said. 'I can't wait any longer for you to open it.'

As she took the gift voucher from the envelope, she gasped, 'Oh, heavens. You knew, all the time. Thank you, darling, but I'm not sure if I can do this.'

'Of course, you can. It'll be fun. Happy birthday, my love. Come on now, let's eat.'

'May I have a look at what you've written today?' asked Shirley later that evening.

Andrew paused, 'No, no, let's leave it for now. I need to look at it again myself.'

Saturday came all too quickly for Shirley.

'Time to go,' called Andrew.

She came downstairs to join him in the hall. 'Are these all right?' she asked, holding out the tracksuit and trainers she was carrying.

'Perfect. Now come on we've a long way to go.'

They made good time and checked into the hotel early evening.

Shirley took some persuading to have breakfast the next morning. She was feeling anxious and hadn't slept very well but Andrew made her have a cup of coffee and a couple of croissants before she drove them to the bridge. She left Andrew at the Visitor Centre.

'Right, Shirley, please fill in this form. It's for the insurance.' said the receptionist. 'Then we'll weigh you. As you know you need the correct bungee cord for your weight.'

Shirley laughed nervously, 'Yes, I've read your notes, thank you.'

She joined the rest of the group for the briefing session. She greeted them and thought how calm they looked. Perhaps she did too but her stomach felt full of curdled milk. It kept erupting into her throat leaving a bitter taste. She swallowed and said to herself, *breathe deeply, relax, shoulders down.* The instructor explained the procedure; they were weighed again by a different operator and assured their equipment would be checked by five individuals before they jumped.

Finally, he said, 'Now, let's go and enjoy ourselves,' and led them up the two hundred and ten steps to the top of the bridge.

As if ... she thought. She had to stop a few times to catch her breath but, on such a bright morning, she had to agree that the view to the river far below was fabulous. They made their way, single file, to the middle of the bridge where she waited her turn to be kitted out. She was tense, she rolled her shoulders and breathed in the crisp cold air. Could she do it? No, she didn't think so. She felt sick. Oh, Andrew, what a present, just supposing it all goes wrong? The waiting was almost unbearable.

Once in her harness, the straps holding her ankles together were attached and final checks made on all the equipment. She closed her eyes, unable to watch anyone else leap from the bridge.

'OK, Shirley, your turn.'

She shuffled along the platform to stand on the edge. 'No, I can't do it!' she gasped, attempting to turn round.

'Yes, you can,' came a voice behind her. 'Look ahead. I'll count down from three and you launch yourself off. Ready?'

Before she could answer, she heard, 'Three, two, one ...' and she was flying, arms outstretched, towards the water below. The adrenalin rush was unlike anything she'd ever experienced; the wind against her face made her eyes water. Seconds later she was bouncing gently up again and saw the boat coming towards her. There was Andrew, who'd persuaded the boatman to bring him, thumbs up and grinning.

'I did it,' she cried. 'Wow!'

'Good on yer, girl,' he shouted.

The boat's crew caught her shoulders and carefully guided her into the boat, unhooked the bungee rope and made for the bank.

'I said you could do it,' said Andrew laughing, 'a real *Voladora*!'

'Once is more than enough,' she replied. 'Never again.'

Over breakfast on Monday, Andrew said, 'I've finished that chapter. When you have a minute, will you read it through and tell me what you think?'

'OK, I'll do it tonight. I've asked several friends round to show them the DVD of my bungee jump but that won't take long.'

Shirley had a good evening. Everyone enjoyed the DVD showing the impressive Middlesbrough Transporter Bridge over the River Tees and marvelled at Shirley's one hundred and fifty foot dive towards the water.

She was in a happy mood when she sat down with Andrew's manuscript. He'd woven an intriguing tale around the legend of the Totonac flyers but she caught her breath when she came to the close of the chapter. He'd described in detail the tragedy of one flyer whose vine had been tampered with and how he had fallen to his death.

She shuddered. 'What if ...?'

Eve

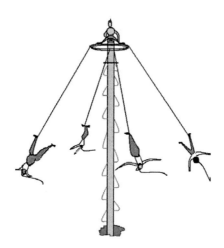

The Promise

Stacey heard her mother call from the hall. 'Is everyone ready?'

With her two brothers, three pairs of stamping feet hurtled down the stairs, out of the front door and into the car.

Traffic built up as her father turned off the main road and drove along a narrow lane leading to Popstone Airfield where the annual August Bank Holiday air show was blessed with a clear blue sky, light breeze and a large gathering of privately owned aircraft.

Stacey was the most enthusiastic. Her hazel eyes darted from one aircraft to another. 'Look, Dad, a Piper Cub, a Cherokee and a Tiger Moth. Oh, hurry up and park, just there by the rope barrier. That's the best spot.'

Doug Thompson laughed and said, 'Hilary, I think we have a pilot in the making. That space will do fine.'

'I think it's stupid for a girl to fly; only boys have the brains for it,' Michael the eldest piped up.

'I agree. Girls should keep to dollies and cleaning house.' Middle son, John, waggled his fingers from his temple and poked his tongue out at Stacey.

Stacey turned from the window and glared at her brothers. 'You're mean, jealous pigs. I want to do more with my time than watch TV and play computer games. Mum says "The world is our oyster". We can do anything we like if we put our minds to it.'

'Rubbish, women can't lift bricks, work cranes, can't ...'

'Yes, we can,' Stacey shouted.

'Enough!' The command left Hilary's lips like a drill sergeant, 'Out of the car, all of you. Michael, John, you get the chairs from the boot; Stacey, the picnic basket. Doug, we'll get the ice creams.'

'Yes, ma'am, at once.' Doug smiled. 'I'm at your command.'

At two o'clock the displays started to zoom around the sky. Some solo, mostly in pairs and then a daring loop performance by a Tiger Moth. It was buttercup yellow with silver wings and Stacey knew that she had found the plane she wanted to fly.

Her brothers were allowed to explore by themselves, but Stacey wandered with her father amongst the high and low winged aircraft. Pilots chatted and held small children up to look into the cockpits.

The Tiger Moth was at the end of a row and Stacey impatiently dragged her father towards it. 'Look, Dad, it's the only one here. Quick! Before he leaves.'

Kevin Walsh, the pilot, leant against the fuselage. He was in his early sixties, tall and with a head of dark wavy hair. He had a square-shaped face roughened by the wind and sun.

'Hello, I'm Stacey Thompson. I was fourteen last week. Can I have a ride in your Tiger Moth?' The words spilled over each other and as she took a breath, Kevin turned to look at her.

Stacey smiled at him, knowing she could charm the devil if she wanted to.

'Well now, you're a bit young for my type of plane. It doesn't have covers over the cockpits and we would have to sit separately, you in the front and me behind. I'm sure your Dad would be very worried about you.'

'Dad won't worry. I'm tall for my age and ...'

'Definitely not, my girl. Your mother would have a fit. Sorry about this, but she's aeroplane mad. Pity my two boys aren't.'

Doug pulled Stacey away but she broke his hold and ran back to Kevin.

'Please, if I can't go for a ride, can I sit inside? I won't touch anything.'

'Is that OK with you, Dad?' Kevin asked.

'OK. Just a sit in.'

Kevin arranged the belts over her shoulders, explained the dials and controls.

'Tell you what young lady. When you reach eighteen come back and I'll give you a ride in the old Moth. I promise.'

'Dad, did you hear? I can come back for a ride.'

Doug shook Kevin's hand. 'Thanks a lot, you've made her day.'

'Happy Birthday, Stacey. It's the big eighteen today.' Hilary Thompson hugged her tall, slim daughter and gave her a package.

Stacey ripped the silver paper from the box. Inside, cradled in yellow tissue was a leather flying helmet and goggles. A card read: *For this weekend – have a great day.*

'Oh, Mum, they're beautiful. Dad has given me the air show ticket.'

A lump lodged in Stacey's throat. Her dream was about to come true.

For the past three years, Stacey and the family had gone to the air show and she had always talked to Kevin after his display. Although she only saw him at this annual event, her enthusiasm had sparked a kinship between them.

But over the past year the Thompson's had faced a crisis. Doug had been made redundant and money was tight. So this year Stacey was going alone.

Soon after the show opened, Stacey parked her scooter at Popstone Airfield. Little had changed since her first visit. The Control Tower and runway had been upgraded, but they still used rope barriers and the planes were paraded in rows.

After the display, Stacey searched for Kevin. She thought it strange that he hadn't been in the air. He wasn't in the parade area either.

Stacey felt frustrated. The outspoken, curly-headed teenager hadn't changed, even though she was now a young woman. She cherished this show day when she could talk mechanics, design and old planes with him.

She knew he kept the Moth in the hanger. Muttering to herself, hoping he was there, she set off across the field to find out. The doors were wide open.

The Tiger Moth was the only plane inside, parked at the back. It was quiet compared to the noise of the showground and as she walked further in it became much darker. She called Kevin's name. The Tiger Moth seemed in order, in fact, the plane looked ready for flight, but Kevin was nowhere to be seen.

Fingering her new leather helmet, Stacey felt disappointed. This was to be *her* special day, *her* special flight. Kevin had promised.

Out of the blue, Kevin was there, walking round from the other side of the plane.

'Are you ready, princess? Today's the day. We've waited a long time for this. I see Hilary bought what I suggested. There's a package in the rear seat for you. Happy Birthday.'

Stacey eagerly opened her present. 'Wow, Kevin, a real leather flying jacket! Thanks a million.' She went to hug him, but he stepped back.

'My pleasure.' He laughed. 'Don't get any bigger, that cost me a whole day's worth of flying lessons.'

The fur lined jacket was a little too large, but strapped in her seat, helmet and goggles on, she felt just like Amy Johnson.

The noise of the engine was exhilarating as they flew up into the sky. Stacey marvelled at the green patchwork fields, threaded by streams. English country villages spread neat and picturesque. There was a cricket match and the players looked like pegs running between the wickets.

Climbing higher, Kevin asked through his mike, 'Would you like to loop, princess?'

'Oh, yes, please, high in the sky, over and over. This is wonderful.'

She felt the power, watched the altimeter rise and saw the world turn upside down. The grace of it was like a ballet as Kevin repeated the loops.

'Would you like to fly her?' His voice sounded like a whisper in her ears. 'You can't do much harm way up here.'

'Can I, just for a little while? You will watch what I'm doing? Take back the controls if I get into a dive?'

'Of course, but you'll be fine.'

Stacey placed her gloved fingers around the control stick and knew this was what she had always wanted – to fly. Above the summer countryside Stacey soared like a bird. She tried to remember all that Kevin had told her and as her natural talent took over, she felt as one with the Moth.

Kevin landed and taxied back to the same place in the hanger.

Standing beside the twin-winged Tiger Moth, Stacey smiled at Kevin. 'This has been the best day of my life.'

'A promise is a promise, princess. This was to be your day to fly. Take care of yourself. It's time for me to go.'

As Stacey walked out into the sun-soaked afternoon, she turned to wave - but he was gone.

She put her new flying jacket into the pannier of her scooter and stroked the soft leather. It was all hers, ready for the lessons she would have one day. As she reached for her helmet dangling from the handlebars, an announcement came over the loudspeaker.

It is with regret that we have to announce the death of one of our pilots, Kevin Walsh, in a car accident on his way to the show today.

Stacey froze, shocked and confused. 'But that's impossible,' she whispered. 'I've just been flying with him ...' Then she remembered his words from long ago.

'I promise.'

Julie

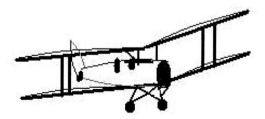

The Crow

We came back from our short holiday; it had been perfect: clear skies, cooling breezes, cropped turf and early summer flowers. But nothing had changed: I felt as though I was at the bottom of a deep pit, and I would never find a way to climb out.

Hal tried to lighten my mood. He made jokes, eulogising how lucky we had been with the weather and the beauty of the Dorset coastline. I tried to respond and forced a smile, but he wasn't fooled.

The next morning I looked out of the kitchen window. There it was, a young crow, unable to fly, with short wing feathers barred with white. It called to its parents and, high up in the oaks, they called back.

We went into the garden. 'Hal, it can't fly! The crows never come down, they won't feed it. What can we do?' I asked anxiously.

'It's better to leave it, Karen. If we interfere the parents will desert it. We'll keep out of the garden today. Give it a chance,' he said.

Give it a chance – what chance? No chance. My hand slid towards my stomach, but Hal was looking at me, so I turned and went into the house.

I watched from the window. The crow, hunched in the border, seemed unaware – unafraid. Then suddenly it spread its wings, raised its head and opened wide its red mouth. It wailed a croak of deep despair as though saying: *I need you. I am hungry. Feed me. Feed me. Love me. Don't desert me. Love me.*

All afternoon its cries of anguish and hunger pierced the walls of our home, echoing my own internal cries of misery and loss.

'Karen, come away from the window, you can't do anything. It's probably the runt of the nest and the others pushed it out. I'm surprised it survived the fall,' he said, a worried look on his face.

'But, Hal, it won't last the night – a fox or that horrible cat, Norman, from next door will get it,' I said, close to tears.

'That's nature, Karen. These things are happening all the time, normally we aren't aware of them.'

His calm acceptance and self-satisfied logic irritated me.

'That's nature,' he repeated, 'the strong survive and the weak die.'

How could he say that? He saw my expression and tried to put his arms around me.

'I'm sorry, Karen …'

I pushed past him and went upstairs.

I was up early and I could hear the crow calling. It *had* survived. I felt vindicated – it would live. It was meant to live. I willed the parents to come down and feed it. All day its cries made me ache inside. Please don't die, I thought. Live – live for me.

It survived another night but now its cries were fewer and weaker. I went outside. It was perched on the back of the garden bench. I crept towards it. It looked at me with wary interest. I must do something, I thought. What?

I went into the kitchen and looked in the fridge. Cheese? Bacon? Tinned dog food!

Tess, the Labrador, looked with interest as I placed some pieces of the dark meat and jelly on a long-handled spoon. It was the nearest thing I had to road-carrion.

'Sorry, Tess, not for you,' I said. She looked disappointed.

I walked towards the crow and slowly moved the spoon forward until it was below its head. A bluish eye looked at me, then it cocked its head and inspected the food. It showed no interest. I slowly moved the spoon up, until the meat touched its beak. Would that tempt it?

I moved the spoon down. The crow raised its head and then, with a piston-like movement, its beak pierced the food. It raised its head and a piece of food was held delicately in its beak, acquired with the skill of a duchess tonging a cube of sugar from a Worcester bowl. It tilted its head back and swallowed.

I was surprised and thrilled. Tears ran down my cheeks. It had taken food. It would live. I held the spoon steady and it ate hungrily but warily, stopping when food stuck around the edge of its beak to bend down and wipe it delicately on the edge of the seat.

I felt proud, justified, I had made a difference. It didn't always have to end badly. I turned back to the house. Hal was watching me from the conservatory door, smiling.

'It ate a lot,' I said excitedly.

'I've been watching. It needs raw food. I'll buy some mince tomorrow.'

We fed it for five days. Each morning it would walk up the lawn, with its old salt gait - we never knew where it spent the night. It was bold and brave, ignoring the squirrels, the other birds; focused on surviving and making contact with its parents.

Each day it seemed sleeker, stronger, more of an adult. It preened and extended its wings, often balancing on one leg and stretching out the opposite wing like a high-wire artist with a feather parasol. It ate the mince and Hal fed it if I had to go out, reporting progress when I returned. I didn't give it a name, or decide if it was male or female – I didn't want to chance fate again.

On the morning of the sixth day it was gone. Had it managed to fly and join its parents? They too had gone. The garden seemed empty without their raucous cries. All day a soft sadness permeated me. Hal looked at me warily. I knew he was worried that this would make things worse.

'Shall I throw the mince away, Hal?' I asked. Then I thought of Tess – how silly of me - of course.

'I'm sorry, Karen. You did your best. I'm surprised it lived that long.' He stopped, realising what he had said. 'Karen, I meant the crow, not …'

'I know what you meant, Hal. We gave it a chance. It may not have survived, but I'm glad we tried. It was lovely being close to it, if only for a few days. It was a privilege.'

I moved closer to him. 'I'm sorry I've been so difficult since … I couldn't accept it, couldn't believe it had happened. All parents can lose their young. The crows have other young and next year they'll be back to make a nest in our oak trees. Life will go on.'

He took my hands. 'And our life, Karen. Will our life go on?'

I moved his hands and placed them over my empty womb. 'I will always grieve for the baby, but I want to try again. I *want* a baby – I *want* to give a baby a chance to live, to grow, to love.'

He held me tight and we both cried. In the distance I heard a crow calling from the nearby wood.

The next year I was sitting in the garden. It was a lovely summer's day. In the pram beside me, shaded from the sun, was our two month old son, little Hal. He was perfect - lovely.

I raised the shade to see his face: skin as delicate as the petal of a peony and dark eyelashes resting on his cheeks. When I look at him I feel my heart will burst with love.

Suddenly the still air was broken by the flashing of ebony wings. I started and leant over Hal to protect him.

A crow, a handsome adult, landed on the back of the garden bench. It looked at me, cocked its head and seemed to glance at little Hal. We looked at each other – I knew it was my crow.

Then it took off – rising strongly with beats of its powerful wings. Calling stridently, it flew away. I was filled with joy as I watched it move through the air. I had given it life – the crow had given me hope.

Vera

Free As Air

When Tessa Musgrove was twelve years old, she ran away from home to join the gypsies.

Understandably, the gypsies did not want her, and brought her straight back in a white Transit van with missing hubcaps.

'It's not all it's cracked up to be, dear,' coughed Mrs Violet Jones, 'the life, that is; you can take it from me. Ran away meself, but no one brought *me* back. Now I've got five kids an' a bloke what's more at home on roofs nicking lead at night, rather than home in bed. Mind you,' she said as an afterthought, 'that's not such a bad thing, come to think about it.'

She bent over the steering wheel in a paroxysm of coughing, and the van lurched dangerously from side to side.

'Is your cough from all that cooking over wood fires?' asked Tessa sympathetically.

'No dear, just the fags. Anyway, I've got a lovely little Calor stove in the caravan. Wood fires indeed!'

Tessa's parents had mixed reactions to her escapade.

'Darling, are you so very unhappy at home to want to leave us? Didn't you think how worrying it was for *me?*' Her mother's face was streaked with tears, and the sitting room floor was littered with small balls of wet, white tissues, like a golf range. 'Just suppose someone had seen you?'

Her father simply asked, 'Why, Tess?' and put his arms round her.

From the safety of his tobacco-smelling jersey she replied, 'Just wanted an adventure - you know, be a bit free, see what it was like, that's all.'

John Musgrove glanced round at the heavily mortgaged house, and at the calendar with the month's activities already blacked in. He thought of what lay ahead, known only to himself, and sighed. Looking down at the top of his daughter's head, he said, 'That's okay, Tess. I understand. Now let's all have some supper. We can talk later.'

Violet Jones left after a cup of tea, with a twenty pound note tucked in her battered brown purse. As the van went down the driveway, John noticed that neither of the brake lights worked.

'You're not just going to leave it there are you, John?' Sandra Musgrove turned to glare at her husband from the quilted dressing-table stool in their bedroom later that night. She had creamed her face and was now working cuticle repair cream into perfectly oval nails.

Her hair, he saw with some sadness, was scrunched up into something resembling a string shopping bag. This hair had been the most erotic thing about her when they'd first met. It hung loose in a heavy auburn curtain; her white shoulders, above the blue evening dress, looked almost too fragile to support it. He had been immediately and irrevocably lost. John Musgrove had a thing about beautiful hair and fragile women.

'Darling, I do think you're getting into a bit of a state about this whole thing. After all, you heard what she said. Just wanted a bit of an adventure. *I* think that shows some ingenuity, don't you - a bit of spark? Didn't you ever want to do something like that when you were her age?' He looked at his wife without much hope. He already knew the answer.

'That is *so* much not the point, John.'

Oh God, she's already copying daytime television, he thought.

'You've no idea who she might have met up with at that place,' Sandra went on, 'dregs of society, drop-outs and no-

hopers, supposing someone had - *touched her?* Had you thought
of that?'

'Pity anyone who tried! She's already top of her karate class.
They'd have come off worse.'

'I really don't understand you, John Musgrove, even after
fourteen years of marriage, I don't.' Sandra's blue eyes held
his, but there was nothing he could say, and so stayed silent.
She was, after all, only telling the truth.

He had thought he'd known what they had both wanted then;
professional status and lifestyle to match. Well, he'd risen to
be Head Planner for the County Council, and with that
position, came frequent invitations on expensive card which
ranged across their mantelpiece. It was certainly what
beautiful, self-centred Sandra wanted.

Then he'd unwittingly accepted an invitation to a seminar,
ambiguously worded, advising on building houses on flood
plains. And Verity had happened.

'John, do meet Verity who is our marketing lead on Social
Planning.'

'Champagne, John? We might as well drink it – it's all
budgeted for.'

Homes Are Us was known to be generous, and surely by
now he could recognise inducement signs? Anyway, the extra
freelancing fee on offer would help pay for some of Sandra's
increasing extravagances. He'd thought she'd liked him. Had
thought it was personal. He didn't know, and was too naïve to
understand what was intended. She had thick long hair the
colour of autumn wheat. At the reception it was coiled and
knotted at the base of her pale neck. At the private suite of
Sandals Country Club, it was loose and heavy in his excited
hands.

*

He now thought back to that time. Beautiful little houses had been built. Laughing brides were swung over thresholds. Babies were conceived. Toddler groups and Neighbourhood Watch had been formed. Parties had taken place and in some of the beautiful little houses, car keys had been thrown into the centre of the wood-blocked floors. A new generation of upwardly mobile income families had grown, were nurtured and a great happiness ensued. All was as free as air, and there was no reason for this pleasant estate not to thrive. *Until the rains came.* And it went on raining. Tubs of sculptured box and orange trees floated down the flooded roads. A rabbit hutch with three frightened rabbits bobbed crazily around in the debris, eyes wide-staring and ears laid flat against their bodies. And the people began to be afraid. After the fear came anger, and questions were asked. Demanded. Someone had to be accountable.

In his house built high and safe on the hillside, John Musgrove knew it would be him.

He knocked on his daughter's bedroom door and went in. She was scrutinizing a map of the world pinned on the wall over her desk. It was criss-crossed with lines in red ink.

'Your next adventure, Tess?' he asked her.

'Well, yes, but not yet,' she replied seriously.

They looked at the map together in silence.

'So where do you plan to start? Big place, the world.'

'Well, I thought, Africa,' she said, chewing the end of her auburn plait.

'Why there especially?'

'It's a nice shape and it's got lots of animals.'

'Better not leave it too long then, you'll need to go before they're all extinct.' He gazed at her solemn face, at inky cuffs and nibbled nails, and felt such a strong tidal wave of love and protection, that he was almost engulfed. He stood looking down at her and placed a buff envelope in the centre of her desk. Inside was a post office book with an entry for one thousand pounds in her name. He knew it could not be traced - even afterwards. There was also a note: This is *Free as Air* money, use it unwisely, but well. All my love, Dad.

'You'll probably need this,' he said. 'It's not everything, but it'll help get things started. Don't open it yet, but keep it safe. It's yours, for your Adventure.'

She said, 'Why don't you come with me? It'd be such fun.'

John Musgrove replied, 'Thanks for inviting me, Tess, but this will be *your* adventure. I may well have a different adventure of my own.' He smiled a little grimly to himself, but said 'Circus is in town next week, but let's not tell your mother.'

Eileen

Water

Pisces

THE VIRGIN SARDINE

Early March sleet smacked the window panes of The Unicorn as the five writers, warm and relaxed after their lunch, toasted Eve with the last of the house red.

'So you're a Pisces,' said Vera, 'I believe one of the negative traits you're supposed to show is being weak-willed. Can't see it myself.'

Eve nodded in agreement as she munched.

'I'm not so sure,' complained Eileen, 'you've eaten two chocolate thins, and one of them was mine.'

'Sorry – but it is my birthday lunch,' replied Eve.

'Tell us a story to show you're not weak-willed,' challenged Julie.

'I'm sure you've got lots of those,' encouraged Elaine.

Eve looked pensive, and then she smiled ruefully.

The other four women leant towards her, and Vera nudged Eileen and winked.

'I was fifteen, home for Christmas from an all girls' boarding school; my grandparents arranged a party for me,' Eve said.

'Many moons ago, then!' interrupted Eileen, still looking peeved from the loss of her chocolate thin.

Eve sniffed and continued, 'I had an admirer, Peter, he was twenty-five. I asked him to come to the party and I was thrilled when he accepted. One up on all the other girls – a real man – not a pimply teenager.

'Romance – romance. Would he kiss me? Golly, I thought. I couldn't wait for the party.'

'Rather naïve, were you?' asked Vera.

'In spades,' Eve replied. 'My grandmother declared the next game would be Sardines. I hid in my grandparents' bedroom. Guess who found me?'

'I bet you tipped him off!' said Julie.

Eve looked at her innocently. 'I can't remember – perhaps. It was wonderful; he put his arms around me and gently kissed me. Lovely! He smelt of man and cigarettes, a sophisticated aroma. I was trembling – excited – my first grown-up kiss.' She stopped.

'Do go on,' said Elaine, 'What happened next?'

'He completely ruined the moment. He tried to put his tongue in my mouth, messed up my first ever 'perm' and started trying to take off my carefully chosen party dress.

'What are you trying to do? I thought. Here in my grandparents' bedroom – sacrilege! He'd ruined my romantic moment – the lout. Then I saw the funny side of it and I started to laugh – I couldn't stop.

'It was like pricking a balloon. The other partygoers heard me and soon the room was a crush of bodies shouting "Sardine! Sardine!" Peter left soon after that – I don't think he fancied playing spin the bottle. I lost my admirer, but thankfully, nothing else.'

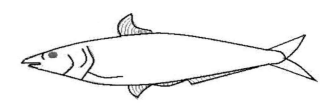

View from the Sea Cabbage Café

I had mixed feelings about visiting Argentina. These people had robbed me of the man I loved. We'd been married only four weeks when Gareth was ordered to join the British Task Force being sent to liberate the Falkland Islands. It was a second marriage for both of us, but he was younger than me – too young to die.

My sister, Myfanwy, and I arrived by air in Buenos Aires on a foggy afternoon in late March for the start of our cruise round the Horn and up to Santiago. Her husband, Bob, was to have accompanied her but a business trip to the Far East had prevented this. I had been persuaded to take his place.

Despite my hostility towards the Argentineans, I found them warm and friendly and the tour guide interesting and knowledgeable. As my sister pointed out, it wasn't their fault the Falklands had been invaded by their military dictatorship. Although I knew this, visiting South America brought the pain and hurt sharply back into focus.

Soon it was time to join our cruise liner and during the overnight sail to Montevideo we met five other Welsh compatriots and were pleased to learn there were more among the many American passengers.

Further down the coast, we called at Puerto Madryn. I had written to relatives of Gareth's in Gaiman, a small town nearby, and we hoped they had received my letter and would join us for tea. Which side of the conflict would they have supported? Although Argentinean they are of Welsh heritage, and, among the casualties were thirty-two Welsh Guards including my husband.

We'd met the Lewis family in Cardiff just before the invasion, when they came over for the Eisteddfod. Myfanwy,

Bob and the two of us had really enjoyed their company. But that was twenty-five years ago and it was with some trepidation that I entered the teahouse where coach-loads of people were milling about finding their places. As a Welsh choir prepared for their recital, the conductor asked if a Senora Emily Lewis was present. Hearing my name, I stood up. I needn't have worried; Gareth's cousins were there and greeted us with open arms. We sat together listening to the warm voices of the choir reminding us of home. Loneliness overcame me as they closed the performance with a stirring rendition of *Land of My Fathers* and I wept for Gareth and all that could have been. The cousins were kind and by the time Myfanwy and I climbed back on the coach, I had recovered. We would correspond and they would visit me in London soon.

That night the weather worsened. Force 6 was forecast. Would this prevent the ship from putting into Stanley? I prayed hard. Part of me wanted an excuse not to visit the Islands but in my heart of hearts I knew, now I was near, that I needed to see where Gareth had died.

We awoke in the morning to find the vessel anchored in Stanley Harbour.

'Offshore islands should belong to the country nearest to them,' declared an American woman as we waited for the tender to take us ashore. *Oh, Gareth, is this what you died for?*

'Does that include Hawaii?' Myfanwy blurted out, her comforting arm around my shoulders. The woman declined to answer.

In the tender I found myself squeezed between my sister and a tall bearded man of about my own age. With a broad grin he apologised for the jam, but I got the impression that he didn't really mind.

'That's all right,' I said, glancing up into deep brown eyes.

Somehow, in the small space, he managed to offer his hand, 'Chris is the name. And,' he added with a twinkle, 'if I'm right, you're Emily with friends in Gaiman?'

'Yes, that's right,' I was oddly flattered he'd remembered. American, I realised, 'and this is my sister, Myfanwy. What are you going to do today?'

'I'm off to Bluff Cove. I have to see those penguins!' he answered as we stood and collected our belongings ready to climb off the tender.

'Oh, so are we.' I gulped. There was a lump in my throat and I wanted to scream - *stuff the penguins - that's where my darling lost his life!*

It was a blustery, grey day but not as cold as it would have been that fateful June. Stepping on to the jetty, I filled my lungs with the sharp, clean air and felt proud, despite my heavy heart, that Stanley had been saved from Argentinian occupation. What could be more British than the scarlet phone box and double-decker bus, or the terraced Jubilee Villas built to commemorate Queen Victoria's Diamond Jubilee?

Our coach took us uphill out of the small town, fifteen miles through a windswept, treeless landscape. We passed low rounded mountains, their foothills littered with extraordinary white stone-runs left by ancient melting glaciers, rocks as large as the sheep which hid amongst them; and fenced-off wayside minefields, a grim reminder of the battle for these islands. On the way, Chris told us he had lived most of his life in the United States but that his roots were in South America.

In a lay-by, we transferred to 4x4s from local farms to descend over the rough peaty ground, covered in scrub to Bluff Cove. As if it were a race between farmer and wife, our drivers drove fast, with engines revving and gears crunching, zigzagging over the uneven soggy land, whilst we hung on as best we could. We arrived twenty-five bone-shaking minutes later. The beach was carpeted with down feathers and populated by Gentoo penguins gazing mournfully out over a smooth grey sea; their stench wafting inland on the breeze. I too gazed mournfully out to sea. Somewhere out there lay *Sir Galahad*. Was this where my beloved should have landed on the final push towards Stanley?

How long did I stand there? In my mind I saw the landing ship, *Sir Galahad*, anchored in the cove, crowded with troops and equipment waiting, waiting, waiting … Should they go ashore at Fitzroy on the other side of the bay, or Port Fitzroy, another name for Bluff Cove? Such confusion fatally delayed the landing. Enemy observers reported their position and at 14.00 hours five Skyhawks came screaming overhead.

I glanced at my watch and shivered – it was two o'clock.

Round they came a second time, the whistle of the bombs and the roar of the exploding ammunition drowned the screams of the injured and dying as fire consumed the vessel; the sea became a boiling cauldron; orange flames shooting skyward and thick acrid smoke filling the air. I saw again the vivid TV news footage of navy helicopters hovering in the blinding smoke to winch survivors from the burning ship.

Why hadn't Gareth been among them?

Everything went black …

'Emily, Emily! Oh, thank God you're all right!' Myfanwy, her troubled eyes watching me, hugged me close.

'Where am I? What happened?'

'Don't worry. You passed out. But you're all right now. We're in the Sea Cabbage Café. Here, have some water.'

I sat up and saw Chris, the man from the ship's tender, hovering anxiously nearby and three ladies behind a counter busily preparing tea for our coach party. The delicious aroma of freshly baked cakes and biscuits filled the room.

'Chris helped me get you here,' explained Myfanwy.

'I'm so sorry. I don't know what came over me.' I murmured.

'Never mind,' said Chris, sitting opposite me, 'as long as you're all right now?'

'Yes, I feel much better, thank you,' I whispered, looking up into his kind concerned face.

Soon the room was full of chatter as our group enjoyed their food in the warm atmosphere. Fortunately, most of them had been too engrossed in the moulting penguins and other wildlife to notice me. Our guide, Colin, came over with a tray of refreshments and asked how I was. I reassured him as he sat down.

'Have you always lived here?' asked Chris.

'Wouldn't live anywhere else,' he said, 'this cove is on my land.'

'Then you were here during the war?' queried Myfanwy.

'Oh, yes! At one time the farm was briefly sandwiched between the two armies. That was pretty hairy. But the most horrendous time was the attack on *Sir Galahad* and *Sir Tristram* here ...' His voice trailed off.

I gasped. I couldn't breathe. I felt I was strangling. Quickly Myfanwy came to the rescue. 'Emily's husband was killed in that raid,' she said quietly.

The two men looked at me.

'Oh. I'm so sorry!' burst out Colin. 'I had no idea.'

Chris reached across the table, taking my hands in his. They were warm, strong and comforting. 'Look at me, Emily,' he said gently.

Looking up, I saw tears in his eyes.

'Now, take a deep breath ... Now another ...'

Gradually I became calmer.

Back on board, Myfanwy, Chris and I watched from the bow as the Captain directed the weighing of the anchor from the bridge. As Stanley receded from view, its lights reflecting in the darkening water, I thought of that sad day, nearly twenty-five years ago, when Gareth's comrades watched *Sir Galahad* being towed out to its final resting place whilst they sang *Land of My Fathers*. We moved slowly out of the smooth harbour and turned south.

'Come on,' said Chris, 'let's go and have a drink before dinner.'

'I'll follow you in a minute,' I replied.

'Sure you'll be all right?' asked my sister.

I nodded.

Without fuss the vessel glided along the coast, past Bluff Cove. The only movement was the luminescent bow wave rippling out around the hull over the still water. I felt cold. The sea would be colder. The warm bar and companionship of Myfanwy and Chris beckoned.

Which country in South America had he come from? I wondered.

'Forget it, Emily, it doesn't matter,' it was as if Gareth were talking to me. 'Wherever he came from, he's a good man.'

'Goodbye, my love, and thank you,' I called softly into the wind. 'Goodbye.'

Eve

Ania

I kneel here on the harbour cobbles, praying for my husband's return. I have not given up praying and begging to God that He has saved our fishermen from the mighty storm and sent their fishing boats home. The other wives have stopped coming. I cannot, for without his return I must do something that will break my heart.

There have been seven days of dark skies but tonight the sky is clear and the stars bright. The moon is full and by its light I can see the tide rising on the great Tiber.

The harbour has an unnatural look – it is empty - only the sound of rowing boats tied to iron rings, tap the wall as the water surges into the bay. The water is black and sinister, like a cloak hiding everything below, hiding the fish and crabs the boys catch to feed the widowed women – of which I may be one now. But this is not enough; we need our men to return. He must come back.

Do my eyes deceive me; is the power of my desire so great that I can see phantoms? No. A fleet is coming in – the second fleet – have they found our men? My hands are shaking and my fingers hurt, for I am squeezing them together in homage to my God. Yet I cannot say the words until I see my Mario step ashore.

The boats are coming swiftly on the tide. Some will moor alongside the wall and others in the harbour. Should I run and tell the women? No! I will wait for my Mario, he may be hurt, may need my help. They should be here, praying as I am. They must hear the sound of the oars, the voices shouting out the orders to heave-to.

The first boat alongside is Crispin's. He does not look triumphant. There are many men, more than the one crew. Does that mean he found them? Found them in that mountainous sea where the waves ride high above their boats when the storms are upon us. I can't see in the dark how many boats are coming in. The second fleet has five and the first fleet seven. There should be twelve. I cannot see how many, my eyes are misty with tears. The plank is coming over the side.

Torchlight is coming from the town. They have been woken by the noise. The old men are hobbling; the young racing in front and the mothers holding their children by the hand. I can see my sister, Beatrice, with her babes and mine. Hurry them fast, they must be here to welcome their father.

Marcus and Lavia are here with me – waiting and hoping for a miracle. One by one the survivors are coming ashore. Their clothes are in tatters and many have bandages over their eyes, for when sea water slaps into them they become very sore. Two of Mario's crew, Leo and Felix, have bandaged hands, probably full of splinters and some truly unfortunate souls, have twisted limbs. They will never sail again. It will be difficult for them to find work. Cripples are not looked upon with any favour. They will end up beggars and their women-folk, whores.

My Mario is not with them.

They could not find him in the sea. Seven boats sailed – none have returned. Seven hauls of fish lost. A good catch will feed the town and what's left is dried and smoked; the women sell it in the markets of Rome.

I am a true widow now.

Beatrice has tried to console me, but she has her husband, a second fleet fisherman to comfort, and two small babes hanging on her skirt to nurse. I must go now and take my children to our home on the northern outskirts. They are but five and four years old and do not understand my grief. I must be strong and not break down until they are bedded. Then I can weep silent tears in the bed Mario and I shared; where he whispered, 'Cleo, my dearest.' And I opened for his love.

They are asleep. I told them that their father would not be returning from the sea, that God had need of him in heaven. Neither child seemed to understand, perhaps because they were so tired. I'm sure in the morning they will have many questions.

Our one room is curtained in half – for sleep and to live. Mario made a window, so that I might sit and look at the countryside. I often dream of living in the villa I can see, owned by the Overseer. In the heat of summer, I imagine my bare feet walking on marble floors and cooling my fingers in a courtyard fountain. But at this moment, I sit here and watch the peach paleness of the dawn bring colour to the green shoots of corn, rising straight like sword tips from the ground. Hedges are showing buds and, far in the distance the hills have a purple tinge; they will need the full sun to brighten their peaks. I want to sit here forever, watch time go by and not have to worry about what I am going to do. There is our hidden box, but that was always meant for when Mario could not sail anymore, when he was old. He is never going to grow old - I will only remember him as my dark-haired, handsome husband with his sunburnt skin a little lighter than the colour of his boat.

I need something of his to hold. There is his shirt on the line. It was Mario's favourite – grey, woven thick cloth. It has a dark hair caught in the open neckline. I shall never see him in it again, never touch his dark hair and never kiss his lips. How am I to bear the pain of losing him? And without him, how can I care for another child, for it is surely coming within a few days.

I can hear the children are awake. They will come to me now for their breakfast. But this day will be different – it is a day of mourning.

Marcus is very like his father; decisive, forceful and the most handsome boy a mother could wish for. He is my first born and I am so proud of him. He is standing with his feet apart, hands behind his back, just like Mario, and has a quiver in his voice. He is declaring that he will look after me and Lavia. He will go fishing with the boys and bring home our food. I can work in the fish smoke rooms and his sister can sweep the floors. He must be so frightened. But I must not show any compassion. I must bow my head and agree.

Little Lavia is staring at him with wonder in her face. Compliance from her is something to behold. She is like me with her fiery temper, dark hair and olive skin. A true descendent of Latium.

It is time - time for me to go into the woods and prepare my place. I have what I need: cloths, knife and blanket. I asked Beatrice to care for Marcus and Lavia, yet not why. She would want to come with me, but I do not want that. This will be a time for me and Mario – me and his memory. I have borne two children, I am not a novice. Yet if anything goes wrong, my babes will become orphans. Children left to be cared for by Beatrice, who could not cope with such a burden. Black thoughts are not for now – I must be strong like my little Marcus – take the responsibility into my hands.

The afternoon is paling. There is no trodden path where I am walking. The Tiber is wide and fast flowing, but soon I shall see a backwater, thickly surrounded by trees and cut by a small island. It is an ideal place for me to make a shelter.

The twigs are burning and the fire is giving good warmth. Mario and I did this when first married, when we were free to run, laugh and love in a bough shelter under the stars. I love him so much. Is his memory enough for me to brave this alone - to give birth? It is, for it will be his hands that rub and ease my pain, his voice will be in my head, encouraging, telling me when the time is right. And the time is now – the first pain has begun.

I see it come as the dawn lightens my shelter. Its cry fills the air. It is a girl. I must rest for a few moments, but when I tend to her and myself, I will count her fingers and toes.

She is beautiful, only her face shows from the blanket. I want to cradle her forever. I want to remember every moment that Mario and I shared when we joined to create such a wonder. He is here, beside me, so vivid and real – yet nothing more than a ghost that must fade before the sun sets tonight.

The fire needs more twigs. 'Mario, can you put them on.' His hands through mine coax the fire for more warmth and I lay down to sleep with Ania – the name we chose many months ago.

The sun is well into the heavens and it is Ania's cry that has woken me. She must be hungry and I have my milk for her now. The fire has gone out, but the air is warm and we are not cold. Come little one, it is time to fill your need.

I am walking in the woods, telling her all about her father, Marcus and Lavia. I am showing her the trees and the river where the fish run deep and are not easy to catch. I keep telling her how much I love her. But the time has come to go and say goodbye, where much love has been shared.

Now I kneel and give prayer. 'Oh God, it is with great sorrow that I pray to You now. But, also, it is with great gratitude that I bless our beloved Pope Innocent III, who has, in his wisdom, made it possible for me to place Ania in his care. I give her to you with my love.'

The water is cold, but I must do this, for Mario and me. 'Do not cry, little one, it is only for a few moments. I ask, O Lord, for your blessing and name this child, Ania. She will have no other name. Amen.' The water is dripping onto her blanket, but the cross is there on her forehead. 'You have been baptised, my dearest daughter, in the Christian faith.'

The drinking houses are closed. The town is asleep. A few dogs are growling. I am creeping in the shadows, peering round corners. I have not seen anyone that could be a danger to us. My weakness is making me shake and I have a sweat on my forehead. Mario would not have let me get up so soon, but I must do this, before I change my mind. It is not what I want. I want to keep her, suckle her and love her. But we would not survive – Marcus cannot fish and Lavia cannot sweep floors. We have only what money is in the box and I can work with only two little ones to care for.

I am here. The convent gates are locked, but the foundling wheel is there, as His Holiness deemed it to be.

The stall is small. She looks so beautiful. I must close the lid and turn it inside. 'Goodbye, my sweet Ania. I pray the nuns will care for you as I would.'

It is done.

My heart will hold you both forever.

'Goodbye, Mario, until we meet again.'

Julie

Breaking the Waves

Trudy pretended to be asleep, the hollow in the sand was comfortable and the late morning sun warmed her skin. The school holidays had started and the family she'd brought down to the beach, from her mother's bed and breakfast, had forgotten about her.

'Our landlady's a Nordic beauty, isn't she?' said the father.

'Bit of an Ice Queen, if you ask me,' said the mother.

'Don't you mean the Snow Queen? She does a good fry up, you've got to give her that!' he replied.

The daughter, who was nine, one year younger than Trudy, didn't say anything.

My Mum, the Snow Queen, Trudy thought. I don't think she loves me. She isn't cruel, like the Snow Queen, but she looks at me and turns away, as though the sight of me makes her sad. Perhaps if I looked like her, she might love me. She always kisses me goodnight, but never hugs me. She doesn't seem to care about anyone, even me.

I wish she'd tell me what my Dad was like. My middle name is Petra, after his name, Peter, but that's about all I know. I've given up asking her. She's always too busy, or she'll tell me later. When they ask me at school, I don't know what to say. Did your dad have black hair, like you? What did your dad do? How did your dad die? Sometimes I wonder if I had a dad. I cried when they said I was an orphan. 'I'm not an orphan,' I screamed, 'I've got a mum.'

In the boarding house, named Pebble on the Beach, Trudy took the phone off the hook, checked her wristwatch and crept up the stairs. She pulled down the ladder. This was the third time she'd secretly climbed into the attic to search for proof that her father had existed, had lived. She was methodically working through the trunks and suitcases stored in the attic since they'd moved, seven years ago.

Hope Mum doesn't wake up, she thought. Her mother had a rest after lunch. In the morning she'd changed the beds and cleaned the rooms ready for the next visitors. Trudy was forbidden to wake her and she had to stay in the house and take phone calls and deliveries.

Trudy looked at her watch - ten more minutes.

It was an old-fashioned, leather suitcase. She opened it. There was a faint smell of ... she wasn't sure, but it reminded her of the beach: tar, seaweed, smooth pieces of glass and sand. A red velvet cloth covered the contents, and beneath it Trudy felt hard lumps and bumps. She lifted the covering. Lying in a jumble were tarnished silver cups and medals with ribbons.

Trudy picked up the biggest cup and tried to read the inscription. She rubbed at the brown stains with the red cloth, and then moved until she was beneath the dirty skylight. She squinted at the engraving through the dancing dust motes.

PRESENTED TO PETER MERIDITH
SWIMMING CHAMPION
BRISTOL UNIVERSITY 19...

My Dad was a swimmer, a champion swimmer! All the cups and medal were his - for swimming. She looked at her watch, then quickly but carefully laid them back in the case. Her heart was pounding as she tucked the cloth around them and closed the case. My Dad was a swimmer.

Trudy sat on the sand, looking at the sea. The waves were gentle, softly rolling in, no white horses, only cream foam stirring the pebbles on the beach. When they had moved to the east coast Trudy hadn't liked the beach: when the tide was in there was no sand to play in and the pebbles hurt her feet. Now she loved it: the soles of her feet had hardened and when the tide went out there were swathes of clean, damp sand, perfect for building sandcastles and moats. Trudy would sit for hours patting the sand around her feet, slipping out of the casts and decorating the sand-shoes with pebbles and silvered shells.

'That kid'll be the next Imelda Marcos,' a holiday maker had said, when she'd completed a row of sand-shoes. Trudy smiled at him, hoping that was a good person to be.

I'll have to learn to swim, she thought. If I learn to swim my Dad will be proud of me. He may be up there - in the sky, with the seagulls. If I learn to swim perhaps my Mum will love me.

Trudy had paddled and played in the sea, but she had never tried to swim. There had never been an adult to teach her. Her mother didn't come to the beach: in summer she was too busy, in the winter it was too cold. Her Mum's parents were dead and her Dad's parents never visited.

Trudy moved to the edge of the sea and looked for a swimmer she could study. The children splashed, jumping up and down in the waves, scooping water in their hands, throwing it over their friends or making circles in the water as they swam in their rubber rings.

Trudy waded out until the sea came up to her arm-pits. A wave surged towards her, lifting her up. She stretched out her arms and rode it, up and down, until she felt the gravel bed beneath her feet.

A man swam past her. She watched him as he forged through the waves, swimming parallel to the pier. He turned around and swam towards the shore. One arm came out of the water, then forward, and his hand, shaped like a spoon, dipped into the sea. Trudy couldn't see what his legs were doing, but he was thrashing them, as if he was having a temper tantrum. My father could swim, she thought. I bet he did it better than you. He was a champion.

Trudy tried to do the crawl, but she sank and came up, coughing and spluttering. Why couldn't she swim? She'd watched several swimmers; she'd tried the breast stroke, but despite moving her arms as fast as she could, more North Sea was swallowed and coughed up. She moved to the shallows, lolling, letting her body roll back and to, with the waves. She was a failure. She hoped her father wasn't looking down. If he was, he would be groaning. If he could be here, she thought, he'd teach me.

She turned her thin body and lined it up with the shore. Her hands touched the bottom and her body floated, weightless. I can pretend to swim, she thought. If I keep one hand on the bottom, make a spoon with my other hand and kick my legs to make lots of foam, I can look as though I'm swimming. She tentatively raised an arm, like the man doing the crawl, stretched it out, dipped it down until it touched the bottom and released her other arm. Slowly she moved forward. By the time she had reached the break-water she was confident enough to move her legs. She imagined the people on the beach must be watching her, they would be saying, 'Look at that girl, she's a good swimmer!'

'Mum, I can swim. I taught myself to swim.' Trudy looked at her mother over the tea-table.

Her mother stared at her. 'You can swim? You can't swim. You need to be taught to swim. Are you lying to me again, Trudy?'

Trudy's face coloured and she hung her head.

Her mother sighed, looked at Trudy and started to clear the table.

Trudy saw pain on her mother's face; she had hurt her, again.

The holidays were coming to an end. There weren't many people on the beach. School would start again in a few days. Trudy lay in the sea, letting the rolling waves sway her body from side to side. The sky was as blue as the periwinkles in the garden. She loved the water moving over her skin, the excitement of the foaming waves as they rushed past. She turned over and lazily pretended to swim. One hand down, one hand up, thrash those legs. She closed her eyes and blew bubbles into the sea.

Suddenly she realised she was swimming! She wasn't touching the bottom. She was free. She could swim. Happiness and excitement shot through her. She leapt up from the water, waving her arms, scaring the seagulls.

'Dad! Dad! I can swim!'

'Mum, I want you to watch me. Promise?'

'I'll watch you, Trudy. But I can't stay long, we've got two new couples arriving soon.'

'Just watch me!'

Trudy ran over the pebbles and plunged into the sea. She stood up, turned and looked back. Then with arms stretched out and palms together, she plunged into a wave and swam out, into the deeper water.

She turned back and looked at the beach. Her mother was standing close to the water's edge, clutching a towel to her chest. As Trudy swam to her she could see that she was crying, but she was also laughing and waving.

My Mum is beautiful, Trudy thought.

She struggled out of the water and ran to her mother, 'I can swim! I can swim!'

Her mother hugged and kissed her, folding her in the towel.

'My Dad was a swimmer, wasn't he?' she asked, shivering as her mother rubbed her dry.

'He was. A marvellous swimmer.'

'What was his favourite stroke?'

'The crawl.'

'Like me?'

Her mother wiped away tears with the towel, kissed her again and laughed, 'He was just like you.'

Vera

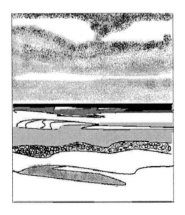

The Luring

Miranda was orphaned when her parents died in an accident off the Galapagos Islands. An Extraordinary General Meeting was held to discuss her future and it was decided to send her to boarding school in England. There were problems - school trunk, name tapes, for, in her case, there was a difference. Miranda was a Mermaid.

The gathered Confluence of Merfolk had reached their decision with difficulty, but agreed finally they had to adapt to survive.

'After all,' said Ariadne, the Chief Mermaid, 'If Selkies can transform themselves from seals to humans, so should we.' The real truth was that she was jealous of Miranda who, at fifteen, was growing daily more beautiful. Ariadne would be well pleased to be rid of her.

Miranda left the following day on a cargo ship bound for Falmouth carrying a load of cowrie shells. The Japanese crew were quiet and polite, and did not question their beautiful passenger as she practised walking with hobbled steps up and down the deck each day. They did admire her swimming prowess when, at anchor, she disappeared over the side for long periods, although they never saw her enter the water or emerge from it, assuming that she used the iron ladder.

'And *don't* sing,' warned Ariadne before she left. 'Last thing we want is for you to lure any of the sailors off the ship before you arrive.' She wanted nothing to hinder Miranda's journey.

Tremedda House, a school for misfits, was set on a hill above the cliffs at Cape Cornwall. Looking out from her dormitory window, Miranda could see Zennor village below and, beyond that the sea. She unpacked her few belongings: the long-handled mirror inlaid with shells, an ivory comb and a shell which you could hold to your ear and hear the waves. And a letter to *Sea-Between*. He was a cobbler, and would be the link between her past and present life, her Councillor and Guide between sea and land.

'Your trunk has arrived and it's all unpacked, my dear.' Matron puffed her way between the beds to the end of the dormitory where Miranda stood. 'So sorry to hear of your tragedy, but we'll do everything we can to help. I must say it's a good thing we're not a school as insists on uniforms,' she added, 'you've got a rather unusual collection of clothes. Wore a lot of long skirts where you came from did you, my dear?'

Miranda turned the full strength of her smile on Matron, and green eyes swimming with unshed tears, she replied, 'Yes, I did rather.'

And Matron was lost.

The School Doctor was next. Miranda wondered what this handsome young man was doing here in a small Cornish practice dancing attendance on spotty schoolgirls twice a week. She also wondered if he could be relied upon for supplying condoms. Ariadne had talked airily about birth control, but Miranda was a little sketchy as to how this applied to mermaids. Looking at her school companions, Miranda thought there would be little requirement, but perhaps he'd have his own supply?

'Er, Miranda isn't it?' he asked the lovely creature sitting before him.

She sat demurely, dark hair in a plait which reached below her waist. She wore a long, green skirt in some filmy material, beneath which her tail fin was invisible.

'So how can I help, Miranda?' he asked, looking as though he'd lost his equilibrium and couldn't believe she was a schoolgirl.

'I would like to have baths instead of showers,' she said, coming straight to the point. 'Since my parents' death, I'm frightened of being in enclosed spaces - like showers - with other people.' She fixed him with a green stare of entreaty, 'I'm sure you understand?'

She knew then from the way he was gazing at her, that he would like to make everything right for her. But she also knew that what he really wanted to do, was unplait her long dark hair and see it cascade over her bare and beautiful shoulders.

'I do not think that there is anything in School Rules or Health and Safety that forbids your taking baths instead of showers, so I will agree pro tem,' he replied stiffly.

Of course he would. He too, was lost. Miranda just smiled.

On Wednesday afternoons, the girls were encouraged to do work 'in the Community', and allowed to catch the bus into the nearby town.

'I'd rather do the mad than the elderly,' Rose Madder had complained to Miranda. 'Last one got me to cut her toenails - like rhino-horns they were, shot off in all directions and one got me in the eye.'

Miranda found the cobbler on her first free afternoon from Tremidda House. *Sea-Between* kept a small shop in the old part of town between Boots and Age Concern.

'I've been expecting you, Miranda,' the soft Cornish voice came from behind a pile of hides at the back of the shop. There was a warm smell of leather, beeswax and saddle soap. 'I have made you these,' the cobbler said, holding out a pair of small, soft, green shoes. 'I need you to hop up here on my work bench and try them on so we can adapt them for your own, er, measurements.' He smiled at her, and walking to the shop door, turned the street sign to 'Closed.'

She slithered up onto the bench, and he fitted the chamois leather carefully over her tail ends.

'There, you look almost human,' he smiled again. Miranda saw in that instant, he'd seen her as a woman, but looking into her eyes, had known she was not. 'And now,' he added briskly, 'I must remember you're a mermaid and I must discharge my duty to you.'

'We'll start with the singing - don't! If you can't get out of it, just try to blend in with the others.'

She opened her mouth to protest, but he forestalled her.

'Pendour Cove has had its fair share of shipwrecks without you adding to it, my lovely. And the luring, Miranda; you must not do any luring.'

She swivelled her elegant length around to face him, and looked at him wide-eyed. 'I wouldn't dream of such a thing,' she said, swinging the long plait indignantly over her shoulder. 'Anyway, there's no-one round here to lure.'

'You're a Mermaid,' he replied flatly, 'and Mermaids will always find someone.'

'You bin buying then?' asked Rose Madder when they met on the four o'clock bus. She eyed the plain brown bag holding Miranda's shoelets with curiosity.

'Just a few bits, nothing much. What about you?'

'No such luck - bin up at Happy Hall, and wouldn't you know, she's only asked for me *special* again. She says I've got such a gentle touch on her feet, and now she don't want anyone else. And now it's corns. What a bummer!'

'What's a *bummer*?' asked Miranda.

'Blimey, where you bin not to know that? Like - *bummer, shite* - you know - *bummer*. Like losing your mum and dad?' Rose said tentatively. 'That's *a bummer*.'

'Oh yes, it certainly was,' said Miranda, feeling her new shoes soft beneath her touch.

As the term went on, Miranda slowly adapted to school life. And the girls came gradually under her spell. Minis were abandoned in favour of long skirts, and they tried to copy her swaying walk and tiny steps. Girls with short hair grew it longer; girls with long hair wore it plaited down their backs. But for all their adulation, Miranda yearned only to swim again and feel the sea caress her body.

The coast path from Tremedda House wound down and away past the ravine where the stream flowed into the sea. By day it was lush with burdock and purple Herb Robert. Long-stemmed whitebells, primroses and violets grew over the path, butterflies spread their wings in the sun on flowering blackthorn hedges. But at night it was different. A fox loped silently past on soft pads; from black trees owls swooped on small mice. But Miranda was intent on her own business. She could smell the sea and hear the waves as they broke against the shore. At last, diving from the rocks she entered once more into her own kingdom, and was happy. Afterwards, coming back up the path, she broke the rules and sang.

Later, Miranda slithered into her dormitory bed. Bright moonlight slanting through the window picked out a small trail of tell-tale sand and shells.

'You got a bloke, Miranda? Don't think I don't notice you sneaking out at night - but don't worry, you're safe with me, I can keep me trap shut.' Rose's eyes, bright with curiosity, peered at her over the bedclothes 'You're a sneaky cow though, how d'you do it under our noses? It's not Barmy Brian as delivers the milk? Go on, tell us it's not him. No, you wouldn't have him. We know he's always on the pull, but he's not in your league. Or - what about that Mathew Trewhella up at Trewey Farm? I seen him at the mobile chippy down Zennor, I'd break the rules for him any day - or night! So go on, who is it?'

But the only reply was a faint and even sound of breathing from the other bed.

The summer was long and hot. Haymaking was well advanced and farmers were hopeful of a record harvest. They worked long into the evenings until the light faded, and then slaked their thirsts in The Tinners' Arms. Walking back from there one night, Mathew Trewhella took the short cut from the coast path up to Trewey Farm. Someone was singing on the path ahead of him. Drawn on, he quickened his stride to catch up with the voice. Had he drunk too much Tinner's Extra? She was iridescent in the moonlight, moving swiftly with small and even steps; her long hair hung wet around her shoulders.

'I'm sorry if I startled you. You have a beautiful voice.'

'Thank you, but I am not in the least bit startled.'

'Have you been swimming?'

'As you see.' She stroked her wet hair with a sinuous movement.

'It's dangerous to swim from Pendour Cove - the rocks - you must be a good swimmer?'

'Of course. Do you swim here?'

'When I have time, yes. It's *my* own place.'

Miranda liked the way he took ownership of the cove. She looked at him standing easily on balanced feet, the blue denim shirt open at the collar showing a brown throat. His hair was fair and curled long at the neck, and his muscular legs were planted firmly astride the path.

What could she do? She was a Mermaid, after all.

'Haven't seen you before - are you working for the summer season round here?' She smiled her Miranda smile. He looked into her green eyes.

'I'm at Tremedda House.'

'The school?' He sounded disbelieving. He paused, then asked tentatively. 'Do you ever get out - like to come out?'

'I am out now, as you see.'

'Well, I mean, on a date - the pictures - *Jaws* is on.'

'Is that *better* than here?'

'No,' he said slowly. 'It could not be.'

'We could go swimming tomorrow night if you like,' Miranda said. 'I would like to swim with you.'

He did not hesitate. 'Then I'd like that too.'

The cobbler found the little green shoes tucked neatly behind some rocks on the shore. And year after year, on summer nights at harvest time, he came down to listen to the two voices singing sweetly far out at sea.

Eileen

141

The Gallery

The gallery was situated across the main road from the Calanova marina's main gate, a splendidly advantageous position as no one going in or out of the marina could miss it. Although small with only one window, the gallery attracted the passers-by with its bright yellow paintwork and the sign which swung in the wind advertising 'Claudia's Art Shop'. It sold a mélange of paintings by a variety of artists; as well as paper, paints, acrylics, crayons and art cards, which drew in many customers.

Claudia was always amazed at the visitors to her little shop and found to her delight that her business did well, not just with passing trade but with regular clients. One man, Paul Rodriguez, in particular, intrigued her; perhaps in his late forties, athletic build, around five foot eight with thick dark hair, large brown eyes, snub nose, generous mouth and, she noticed, good hands.

He had bought a small painting on each of the three occasions he had visited her gallery. Yesterday, he asked if she could take paintings to his apartment and, if he liked what she chose, he would pay cash on the spot. He explained he needed a substantial amount of artwork to decorate the walls of a large block of apartments he had just acquired, intending to let them furnished. Claudia thought the request rather odd, but realising that the arrangement could be lucrative, she agreed. This evening she would take one of her many seascapes.

Claudia pulled up outside the block of new apartments overlooking the bay, high above the town. She retrieved the picture from the boot of her small Fiat Cinquecento, walked to the entrance and, selecting a bell, she rang, waited, rang again, waited and again rang the bell.

'Ah! Welcome, Claudia,' came a deep voice over the intercom. 'Please come up to the top floor, the penthouse suite.'

As Claudia emerged from the lift, Mr Rodriguez came towards her and took the painting, wrapped in a piece of cotton.

'Follow me,' he said and strode off through the entrance a few yards from the lift.

Claudia followed him into a spacious elegant room with a wall of windows looking out to sea.

'What a wonderful view. I can see why you purchased this particular property, Mr Rodriguez.'

'Call me Paul. Sit over here on this sofa and I shall have a look at what you've brought for me.' Paul uncovered the painting and placed it on an easel in a corner of the room. Barely glancing at it he returned swiftly and settled in an easy chair opposite Claudia. 'I approve of your choice and will pay the asking price for the painting. Now, what would you like to drink, Claudia?'

'I am pleased that you approve of my choice of the seascape. The price is quite reasonable at two hundred and fifty Euros and I should like a gin and tonic with ice and lemon, thank you.'

Three hours later Claudia returned to her own modest apartment at the other end of town, having spent a surprisingly enjoyable evening with Paul over dinner, served on the terrace by a quiet and deferential butler, who, at the end of the meal, placed a small tray in front of her on which lay a buff envelope. She glanced across at her host and found him looking at her intently, but he merely said, 'For the painting, thank you'.

Over the next four months, Paul telephoned asking Claudia to take him a painting, often giving her carte blanche to choose the subject. It always followed the same routine: he placed the painting on the easel; she sat on the sofa looking through the window out to sea and he sat opposite and talked with her for a few minutes whilst they sipped their drinks. Dinner followed, served by the butler, and the buff envelope containing the payment for the painting was placed on a tray in front of her at the end of the meal. Claudia began to look forward to these meetings, and found that Paul was not only well read, but had travelled extensively and was knowledgeable on many things.

If she were truthful, she was drawn to this charming man with his magnetic personality, there was a dangerous quality about him that fascinated her. He enquired about her past and asked little personal things, but he always avoided talking about himself. Claudia was happy and relaxed; it had been a long time since she had been in such an engrossing relationship.

Then everything changed.

One evening, Paul, as usual, put the painting on the easel but, instead of asking Claudia to sit down; he pressed a button on the wall. A panel slid back to reveal another room; sumptuous with a canopied four-poster bed. It was dimly lit and he beckoned her forward.

'Wait here, my darling,' he whispered closely behind her and placed his hands on her shoulders.

She took a sharp intake of breath. Was this really happening? Mesmerised by the colourful play of light from the aquarium set into the far wall, it seemed only seconds before she heard the door click behind her. She turned to face Paul, a naked Adonis, smiling at her.

'I think this is what we both want,' he said, taking her hand and leading her towards the bed. Claudia gasped as he started to undress her, slowly, slowly, arousing her desire.

Hours later, saturated with love-making, Claudia reached out for Paul but he was not there. Sitting up, the sun streaming in through the window, she called out, 'Paul, Paul darling, where are you?'

'I'm here, my love,' he turned from the window, 'waiting for you to wake up.'

She opened her arms to him. 'I need and love you, so much,' she said.

And so the months went by. Claudia still took paintings and received buff envelopes, now delivered to the gallery by the discreet butler, the morning following the visit.

One morning Claudia arrived at the gallery to find a message requesting her presence that afternoon at the penthouse.

She arrived at three o'clock to find the main door to the apartment block ajar. Stepping out of the lift she found the door of the apartment also open. Entering, she came face to face with the butler holding a buff envelope which he handed to her and then retreated to the back of the room. An immaculately dressed, white haired lady sat upright in the armchair opposite the sofa.

'Sit down, my dear,' the elderly lady spoke softly with a foreign accent. 'I am sorry to bring you here today but it is the only way. My son, Paul, came here from Argentina to recover from a tragedy. A few weeks ago, Juan, our family retainer, rang and told me how Paul had met you. You see my dear, you have a striking resemblance to my daughter-in-law as she was two years ago before the car accident - Maria was very badly burned. Fortunately, the children were not in the car with her. Now Maria is dying in hospital and Paul has flown to be with her and will not be returning.

'This can't be true,' Claudia gasped in disbelief, 'we were so close. He would have told me. I need to speak to him; be with him.'

'That is not possible, my dear,' the old lady said gently.

'I love him. I adore him. I need him.'

'His family needs him now. Love is not always forever. In time you will meet someone else. No future happiness can be found with my son. I am truly sorry, my dear.'

Numb with shock, Claudia stumbled from the apartment. How could he have deceived me? she thought, I cannot believe, after all we've had that I was just a substitute.

The door closed behind her.

Elaine

146

Sun

Leo

THE CHAIR IN THE WINDOW

It was Julie's birthday lunch at The Unicorn. The sun was shining, as it should on a Leo.

Toasts had been toasted and the five writers drained their glasses and moved onto coffee and petits fours.

'Are all Leos bossy?' asked Eve, looking at Julie.

Julie, about to bite into a chocolate truffle, raised her eyebrows. 'You don't think I'm bossy, do you?' she asked.

There was a pregnant silence.

'You do have strong opinions,' said Elaine diplomatically, 'but that's a good thing.'

Julie munched her chocolate.

'Has your bossi … I mean assertiveness, ever got you into trouble?' asked Eileen.

Julie swallowed and then nodded.

The other four women lent forward, smiling in anticipation.

Tony and I were on a motorbike holiday. We arrived in Liege, Belgium, and Tony wanted to find a hotel in the centre of town.

"No," I said, "we'll find a romantic pension near the river."'

Vera sniggered and Julie glared at her.

Tony sighed and put his helmet back on. After several detours, on crossing a bridge, we saw a pension on a road bordering the river.

"That one looks nice, Tony," I said, pointing to an auberge with a large, downstairs window. He nodded but made no comment. "I've done all the bookings this holiday, you go this time. You can try out your French."

'He sighed and walked across the road, leaving me on the pillion seat. Mmmm, I thought, he looks like Arnold Schwarzenegger in his black leathers and high boots. He pushed the door open and disappeared inside.

I looked at the river: the evening sunlight was dancing on the water and swallows skimmed its surface. I looked back at the pension – where was the man? Honestly! I walked towards the door, helmeted and booted, dying to get my leathers off and have a shower. Muted sunlight was reflected back from the window, and as I came closer, I saw in the window, in front of a red satin curtain, a chair! A chair for someone to sit on!

The door was open and I rushed in – where was my husband? Tony was in conversation with a scantily clad blonde; they were having difficulty in understanding each other.

"No! No!" I hissed to him.

"Julie, I'm quite capable of booking a room," he said testily.

"No! No! You don't understand. There's a chair in the window!"

He looked at me in astonishment.

I took my helmet off. The blonde gaped at me. We all looked at each other. Realisation dawned, and we simultaneously burst into laughter.

Muttering apologies we made a hasty retreat, got on the bike and roared away from the romantic red-light district.'

Sunlight Training

Wilf shuffled for a space in the coal miner's lift. This was his last ride up. Never again would he taste the coal dust or joke with his mates deep in the bowels of the earth.

The government had won. He was redundant - too old to retrain. But how long would the pay-off last? How long before he'd have to ask for social benefits? Could he face that? No. He would sooner jump back down the shaft than face that humiliation.

When Wilf reached his two-up, two-down mid-terrace house, he stood outside, reluctant to go in. Shame stood alongside his anger. He'd been bottling up his feelings for the past two weeks, since he'd opened the letter passed to him by the pit manager.

The house was empty; it always was when he was on the early shift. God, how was he going to face the pitying glances from the other men's wives? He put the key in the lock and went in. He would go straight to bed, then there was no chance of seeing anyone until tomorrow. It would give him a few hours to adjust. Adjust! Who was he kidding?

Wilf didn't sleep. He lay there thinking about the pit and about money, listening to the tick of the alarm clock. At last the shrill ring sounded, four o'clock, time to get up. But it wasn't necessary and it wouldn't be now until the day he died.

The sound of footsteps on the stairs told him his daughter, Molly, was going to make the tea. She knew there was no reason to get up so early now, it was just habit.

He pushed back the covers; *I can't stay in bed another minute.* It was a luxury he had never known and he didn't intend to start now. His feet touched the rag rug and he stood up and turned on the light. What was he going to wear? Not his miner's clothes. He opened the wardrobe door – there was his dark suit for funerals, his sports jacket and grey trousers he wore when he went to the Tattersley Miners' Club. It would have to be the greys. He opened the chest of drawers and took out a white shirt, socks, vest and pants and laid them on the bed.

When his Hilda died, Molly, who had recently been widowed, gave up her rented house and moved in with him. The only awkward thing about it was that he had always washed downstairs. Standing half-dressed at the scullery sink, with Molly around, was a tad embarrassing. So he'd decided to get a plumber to put a wash basin in his room and then life carried on much the same.

Now he filled that basin with hot water, lathered his face and shaved. Washed his face and neck and dried with a coarse towel. He took his false teeth from a glass of diluted bleach and rinsed them with cold water.

It was strange slipping his arms into a cotton shirt, instead of the dark flannel. He tucked the tails inside his trousers and buttoned the fly; then picked up a shoehorn to help his feet into his best shoes. He always polished them to a brilliant shine after every outing, so at least he had one job to do every day now.

As he passed the mirror on the wardrobe door it reflected a sight never allowed in the bedroom - his dull black work boots. He felt choked, almost bereaved, for his life now gone. He wiped his eyes with his knuckles.

It was time to go and face Molly.

'Good morning, Dad. We're a pair of dafties, getting up at this hour. We could both have had a lay-in. Still, I've made the tea. Sit down.'

Wilf sat in his usual chair, but he felt uncomfortable. What could he say to Molly? They usually only grunted at each other

- he would have drunk his tea, picked up his sandwiches and left.

'Thanks.' He looked round the room. It hadn't changed much since he'd carried Hilda over the threshold forty years ago. This was where they lived – he called it the kitchen, Molly called it the living room. There was the mahogany table and four chairs, sideboard and two stuffed green armchairs. The only additions to mark the twentieth century, was a stereo radio and a colour telly. He had felt that Molly deserved some modern pleasures when she moved in.

'Do you want any breakfast, Dad?'

Wilf looked at her and smiled. 'Why not? I've plenty of time now.'

'Bacon and egg?'

'It's not Sunday, Molly. I don't know. What are you going to have?'

'Oh, I just have toast and Marmite.'

'Then, I'll have the same.'

Molly went out into the scullery and Wilf heard her strike a match and then the rattle of the enamel grill tray.

It was only five o'clock. What was he going to do all day?

Molly called, 'Dad, if you have time, there's a bit of veg left in the shed, can you get it, I want to make a stew.'

Wilf didn't answer.

'Dad - did you hear me?'

'Yes. I suppose so. When do you want them?'

'By half-past seven. They have to simmer for several hours so we can have dinner at one o'clock.'

This was a new world for Wilf. Doing shift work had meant he ate either before or after a shift. Now he could have three meals a day sitting with Molly. What were they going to talk about? She didn't want to hear about the coal face or smirking men laughing at tales that weren't fit for women's ears.

'Right then, straight after the toast.'

Molly came back and put two plates on the table and sat down.

'Gwen at the corner shop is on holiday this week. I said I would help out. I have to be there at eight. Will you be all right?'

Wilf felt like a small boy. How had he gone from a miner, who risked life and limb year after year, to a dependent who couldn't be left for a few hours?

'I think, Molly, I can manage not to fall over or hurt myself. I've been doing it ever since I went to work nearly fifty years ago. Don't start fussing now.'

Molly sighed. 'Sorry, Dad, but ... well, this is all new to you ... I mean, having nothing to do.'

Nothing to do!

Wilf let these three words roll round in his mind. They horrified him. 'I'll go and get the veg. You get yourself ready. I'll be fine.'

The sun was climbing over the housetops that backed on to his row. Normally, he would only have had this fresh air walking to the pithead. He breathed in. The air felt cold slipping down his throat, stinging with pinpoint jabs. He closed his lips tight, then opened and breathed in again. This time he knew what to expect and enjoyed the sensation. He did it several times more. He would remember this as the first new experience of his retirement.

'Dad, can I have the veg, time's getting on.'

Wilf waved, 'Coming.'

After Molly left the house it was very quiet.

Sitting in his chair, the one to the left of the fireplace, he pondered whether to turn on the telly. Morning programmes were for the women or schools. But what else was there to do? Hilda had kept house and he'd earned the money. It was as it should be, as had his father and his before him.

Wilf turned the television on and a news reader filled the screen. He tuned to another channel – an advert for grass fertiliser, demanding that the viewer tend their gardens with weekly nourishment as spring was round the corner. The screen flicked to Stork margarine – two young women trying to tell the difference from butter. He turned it off.

They didn't have much grass, just a small patch to sit on in the back. It always looked weedy and those wretched daisies and clover made up most of it anyway. Perhaps, as he had time now he could make an effort to give Molly something nice to sit on. Do a few flowers in a border. He had always grown veg – Hilda had insisted; said they tasted better than those from Greenfingers in the High Street.

After a cup of chicory-flavoured coffee, Wilf thought about the grass again. It would be a token of his appreciation, Molly never asked him to do much, just the jobs she couldn't manage.

Ten minutes later, Wilf locked the front door and set off for the local garden nursery. He reckoned it was about a two mile walk – another first for him – his usual distance was the half-mile to the club for a pint or the same to the pit.

He was out of breath by the time he arrived at Snelgrove Nurseries. It was surrounded by a privet hedge with a wooden gate anchored open. In the centre was an oversized shed with a sign saying: *Everything you want for your garden – Come on in.* That sounded like a good invitation, so he did just that.

'Good morning, sir. If there's anything you can't see, just ask. I'm Charlie.'

Wilf looked at the shelves – bottles, cans and plastic containers stood like soldiers in rows. Watering cans, netting and plant pots covered the floor, leaving barely enough room for him to walk round.

'I'm looking for grass fertiliser,' said Wilf, twisting his neck to try and locate what he wanted.

'Third shelf on the left behind you.'

'Thanks.'

'You new to the area?'

Wilf wanted to laugh at that. 'No. Lived all my life in Tattersley.'

'Just retired, then?'

'Well … yes, I suppose I am.'

Wilf's life crowded in on him. No, he wasn't retired, he was unwanted. There were years left in him to work the pit, but they'd said no. *Be a good man and take the money – sit back and enjoy retirement.* He didn't want retirement – he wanted to work.

Suddenly the shop seemed to shrink and close in on him. 'I'll just go and have a look outside – be back in a minute.'

Wilf wasn't really interested; it was just an excuse to get away from the man. But as he walked, he noticed the shrubs and plants along the paths. They added colour amongst the green leaves – new life struggling to grow – waiting for those keen gardeners to pluck them from the trays and set them into the earth; waiting for gentle rain and warm sun to make them blossom. These thoughts chased away Wilf's dark moment and he wandered amongst the foliage enjoying it far more than he would have ever thought.

After much deliberation, Wilf took a tray of polyanthus, four rose bushes – one of each colour – and pansies back into the shop.

'That's a good start for the season, sir. Did you want the grass feed?'

'Yes, please.'

The man came round from the counter. He limped, much the same as Wilf did when his knee ached.

'A touch of arthritis, I'm afraid. Standing a lot plays it up.'

'That makes two of us. Got mine down the black hole.'

'This isn't a large nursery to run, but I think Old Father Time is trying to tell me something. I've run this place for ten years single-handed, since my Doris passed away, but I think now's the time to seek a little help.'

Wilf nodded, understanding that both of them were suffering, but in different ways.

'I didn't want to give up either. The pit was my world, my life, like gardening is yours. Ageing can be a bum of a cross to bear. This is my first day of *retirement*. They think they are doing me a favour, but they're not. I *want* to work.'

The man nodded. 'A bum cross to bear,' and tapped in the prices of Wilf's goods.

'Cheque or cash?'

'Cash. Is taking cheques a good idea?'

'Latest thing now. The white collar workers are all being paid that way.'

'Oh.' There didn't seem anything else to say.

Wilf parted with his money and realised he wasn't going to be able to carry it all home.

'Stupid me. I can't carry that lot two miles. I'll have to come back this afternoon for some of it.'

'You don't have a car then?'

'No. Never had a use for one - shift work doesn't lend itself to gallivanting about.'

'Sorry, I don't deliver. Although ... what if I come after closing time?'

'It would be a help. Sure you don't mind?'

'Take what you want for today and I'll see you later with the rest.'

Wilf showed his gratitude with a smile. '46 Wheelers Terrace, half way along on the left.'

He picked up the box of grass fertilizer, tucked it under his arm and waved goodbye.

At six o'clock, Wilf heard a knock on the front door.

The garden man stood with the tray of pansies in his hand. 'As promised, all goods delivered as ordered.'

'Come in. We'll take them straight through to the back.'

Molly was filling the kettle when both men came into the kitchen 'What's all this about, Dad?'

'This is Charlie, from the garden nursery. He's delivered the goods I bought this morning. It's for a little gardening job I have in mind. Charlie, this is my daughter, Molly.'

'Nice to meet you, Molly.'

'And you, Charlie. This is kind of you.'

'Cuppa when we've finished?'

'Five minutes, Dad, and it'll be ready.'

Wilf put the rose bushes down by the shed. 'Here will do for now. Thanks for bringing them.'

'Glad to help.'

Wilf held his arm out, indicating the wooden bench. 'It's still pleasant, shall we have our tea here. I'm Wilf by the way.'

They sat quietly, looking at the garden.

'A fair size plot,' Charlie commented. 'I see you grow your own veg, and this is a pleasant bit of grass to rest your feet on. South facing too, but not enough to keep you busy all day.'

'No.'

The man's remark dug deep, emphasising the grudge that lodged like a stone in his belly.

'I've been thinking this afternoon about my business. If I had someone to help out, I could advertise a delivery service. What would you say to a part-time job?'

Wilf didn't answer.

'Sorry, I shouldn't have jumped in like a bull in a china shop.'

'No. You just took me by surprise. A part-time job? But I'm no expert on gardening. True, I have always turned my hand to this bit, but help with your lot ...'

'What you do here is no different, not really, mine's just bigger. Whether you grow one carrot or a hundred, the way you do it is the same. I could give you some training. Especially on the bits you might be dodgy with.'

Wilf couldn't think clearly. 'I don't know. Training you say? Like, teaching me the ropes?'

'Yes, and at the going rate per hour.'

'I don't want a charity handout.' Wilf's voice had a bitter note to it.

The man ran his fingers through his sparse grey hair. 'Look, Wilf, there's no charity here; a good day's work for a fair day's pay. You help me and I can help you.'

Wilf sat quietly and thought for a moment about the man's offer. He had worked hard in the darkness of the pit to earn his bread. This was a chance to work in the sunlight to keep that bread on the table. He could breathe in the fresh air each day, as he had this morning. Cleanse his lungs of the black dust. He would be out of Molly's way; give the house to her like she was used to. He could look his mates in the eye when he went to the club for a drink. Buy his round, as he always had.

He was worth training?

Wilf smiled, thinking of that upstart in the pit office.

Straightening up, he squared his shoulders. 'I'll give it a go, Charlie. Thanks for the offer.'

Charlie held out his hand. 'Done. See you tomorrow at nine o'clock'

As promised, Molly came through the kitchen door carrying a tray. 'Tea's up, boys.'

'Oh, I think we can do better than that,' laughed Wilf. 'Bring out that whisky left from Christmas. I've got a new job to celebrate. Charlie's going to train me up to be a garden salesman!'

Julie

The Hateful Sun

I hate the sun.

I don't hate all suns: I love the winter sun, welcome in the short days of the year; low in the sky, its pale rays cast long shadows in the early afternoon, creating new scenes from well-worn vistas. I love the spring sun, opening the crocuses and releasing their warm, acrid perfume for the sleepy bees, who make golden Jacobean pantaloons from their pollen.

The sun I hate is the mid-summer Mediterranean sun, its great yellow disc beating down on parched lands – a remorseless, mocking, unforgiving sun.

It was the summer holidays and Mark and I were in Crete for the whole six week school break. It was August. We'd rented a villa - a cottage near the beach. I loved him passionately: his sharp mind, brooding, handsome face, lean responsive body and his absorption in his art – painting.

Mark worked in the mornings, rising early at first light. As I lay in our bed I would hear him muttering, swearing, and moving around the room where he had set up his easel. I could see him in my mind's eye as I lay in bed: the movements he would be making, the way he worked the oils onto the canvas, and how he would stand back and stare at his finished work. Then I would usually hear the sound of metal on canvas as he attacked and obliterated the picture. Rarely would I hear a choked cry of triumph. Then I would hug myself, thrilled that he was satisfied with the work he'd done, and I knew for a few days he would forget his painting and we would live for each other.

This was our third year together. I taught - he painted. I earned the money, he allowed me to keep him in food, drink, oils and canvases. He was mine - my passionate, brooding lover – he was what I wanted.

After four weeks on Crete I was tanned, my hair bleached gold by the sun. I was happy – happy to be alone with Mark, our solitude only broken by visits to the market for food, the odd meal out and perhaps an evening drinking grappa with our neighbours. When Mark was painting I swam, cooked, made friends with the children, read the set books for the next academic year, and wrote to friends back home. I was happy, contented

I got up, it was nine and the sun, the golden sun, was beating down and already its heat had lifted resinous oils from lavender and marjoram planted outside the windows of the cottage. Their sharp fragrances cleared my head as I leant out of the window, smiling with pleasure at the blue sea, glinting below.

Mark had been working for three hours. I made coffee, humming to myself, and wandered into his room.

'Coffee, Mark?'

He looked at me with unseeing eyes. I wasn't there - he was in another world. The canvas, which had been a success the night before, was scraped clean, only a few smears of paint remaining.

I gasped with disappointment – disappointment for him. 'Didn't work?' I asked tentatively.

With an expressionless face he said, 'It's no good, Joanne, you'll have to go.'

Go? What was he talking about? I stared at him, he stared back, his face telling me nothing.

'Go? What do you mean, Mark?'

'I can't work with you here. You'll have to go. You're too … too clinging, too smothering. I need to be free to paint.'

Pain wracked through my mind and body, leaving me breathless and sick. I never understood why this handsome, sexy, talented man loved me. My nightmare was that he would leave me. My nightmare was confirmed.

Anguish must have shown on my face, for he frowned and said, 'I'm sorry, Joanne. I love you, but I need my own space. You're always around, it's too claustrophobic. I need my freedom.'

I couldn't find words to express my despair. I stood there, tears runnelling my cheeks. I turned into the bedroom and collapsed on the bed weeping. The sun beat into the room, taking away the freshness and hope of the day.

When, exhausted and red-eyed, I went back to his room it was empty. I found a note in the kitchen:

Joanne, I've gone to arrange a flight for you. I will stay in Crete.

That was all – nothing more. I clung to my one hope: he said he loved me. I pushed open the door. The sea was blue and calm and the hateful sun seemed to mock me with its fiery, yellow eye.

I returned to work – to the school – to the children. I was hollow inside and every night as I clutched a pillow to me, the hollow would fill with pain and overflow with desolation. I loved him so much, I ached to see him, hear him - touch him.

On a Friday night in December I was getting ready to go out with friends from school. It was only the second time I'd been out with them since the summer. The last time we went to a country pub and there was a folk group; everyone was friendly. I hummed as I looked in the mirror, flicking on mascara.

The phone rang.

'Joanne?'

It was Mark. My throat tightened and I could hardly speak.
'Yes.' I whispered.
'I'm here for a few days – I'd like to see you. Can I come over?'
'Now?'
'Yes. Are you going out?'
'No! No! Come over.' Happiness welled up inside me. He was back. He'd come back to me.
We had one night and one day together – we spent most of it in bed. Then he left. Nothing had changed.
'Please stay, Mark – I love you!'
'I can't.'
'Why? Why can't you stay. You said you loved me.'
'I do, but I need my own space to work.'

A pattern emerged. Months would go by. I would slowly rebuild my life and the pain would lessen. Then the phone call, the meeting, the same heady passion, the building-up of my hope, the devastation when he left.
At school I made friends, my career moved forwards, promotion, greater satisfaction and more money. But no romances. I chose to have intermittent days of passion and despair with Mark rather than look for a new relationship with another man.
The time between visits became longer: six months, a year, two years.

I was twenty-nine, a newly appointed deputy head of a large, mixed comprehensive school. It was exciting, fulfilling – I knew I was appreciated by the children and the staff.
It was autumn half-term; I was packing for a short holiday in France with friends. The phone rang.
'Hello, Joanne, it's Mark.'

'Oh!' At the sound of his voice time slipped backwards; all the same feelings which I thought had lessened reappeared as strong as ever: I felt breathless, my heart pounded and my insides melted with longing and desire.

'I'd like to see you. Could you come down to Dorchester for a few days?'

I was confused – my holiday, promises made to friends. I was torn, but then I imagined his face, his eyes looking at me – wanting me.

'Yes, I'll come, Mark.'

It was drizzling as we walked over the downs. I talked about the school, the children, about my plans, the difference I wanted to make. I'd never talked to him like this before – I'd always listened.

He wasn't interested. He wasn't bored – he just wasn't listening. He turned to me. I looked at his face. I saw him afresh, as though I hadn't seen him before. A stranger. He was handsome, but his expression was sour, with lines pulling down his mouth.

I thought of the children at school, laughing with me at some silly joke I'd told them; I thought of the camaraderie of the staff room before school starts.

'Joanne, I still love you. I've decided to come back.'

'Come back? Come back to me?'

He nodded.

I felt disbelief and then ... a new feeling welled up inside me. He saw me smile and moved towards me. I pushed him away, for what I felt was not love for him, but a sense of freedom as I realised it was over. I didn't love him. I didn't want him. I was free.

'I'm sorry, Mark, you're six years too late – I don't love you any more.'

*

After half-term, when I returned to work, I felt as though iron shackles had been struck from my legs. I floated on a sea of optimism and hope. I looked forward to work, friendship, freedom and, perhaps, love.

I still hate that burning Mediterranean sun; it reminds me of my other self, a self I feel ashamed of, a bondswoman, a slave to a one-sided love. I realise my hate of the sun is irrational and that when that hate fades, I will have forgotten him completely and I will have forgiven myself for my weakness.

Friends are planning a trip to Turkey for the summer half-term. They are renting a villa, they want me to make up the party to ten. I know the Head of Music wants me to go; he's asked me out, but so far I've refused. Dare I go? Dare I fall in love again? Can I fall in love again? Will the powerful sun bring back my old longings and desires? Do we ever change?

Vera

Turning the Tables

Anne Thornton had always found it easier to agree with her husband, even when he was wrong. She'd grown expert at subtly persuading him to change his worst ideas, like the time he wanted to take early retirement to run a country pub.

'Darling, that would be wonderful,' she'd responded, 'and it would mean we'd see so much more of each other, working side by side, seven days a week. Of course, I'd do the cooking and you'd be chatting to all the interesting village locals over the bar. Lot of listening there,' she'd added quietly. If it was one thing Roger hated, it was listening to other people. She knew that she usually got her own way in the end without him realizing it. That is, until now. This new thing had been sprung on her and she could see no way out.

Anne had needed to adapt her life after Roger officially retired from his job as financial advisor in a City law firm. Where once he had safely been on the eight-fifteen train from Brimley, now, he was around all day.

'Why on earth have you got the spice rack so far away from the rest of the stuff, Anne?' he'd demanded on his first week home, when she'd returned from her stint at Age Concern. 'Anyway, I've reorganized the kitchen cupboards - you'll find it much more convenient.'

He looked so pleased with himself that she hadn't the heart to be angry. She would just move them surreptitiously back to where she wanted, bit by bit. What did worry her was that he hadn't found any outside interests of his own.

'Stuffy lot up at that Golf Club,' he'd muttered, after going to the Introductory Membership Day. 'Don't want to waste my time trailing round with a pack of old boys talking about birdies and putters and whatnot.'

'Roger, you can hardly say that after one short morning. Why not go another time and meet some different people?' She felt an opportunity slipping away.

'No, Anne, I'd much rather spend the time with you,' he'd replied. 'After all, isn't that what being retired really means; the chance to be together more?' He went on before she had a chance to reply, 'Let's go to that new garden centre tomorrow, get some cheery plants for the garden. I fancy some bright red geraniums instead of those dreary grass things we've got now.'

'But it's my Age Concern morning tomorrow, Roger. All the dates are on the kitchen notice board, and Mrs Tuffnell relies on me.'

'Takes advantage, more like,' he grumbled. 'Woman's never there - too much of this volunteering stuff if you ask me. What's for supper?'

That was why she was so pleased he was going up to London that momentous day; so pleased to see him in a white shirt and dark suit that she didn't recall where he said he was going. Anne invited her friend Liz for lunch, as she knew Roger would be out. They had never got on, and it was better this way. With hindsight, Anne realized she should have taken more interest. Later that evening, as the sun was casting shadows across the lawn, Anne laid a cold supper on the white garden table. She felt a rush of fondness looking up at the square family house where they'd brought up Emma and Peter. She'd had a lovely day. Liz cheered her up and she felt a sense of space that had been missing. Up in her bedroom, she hummed softly to herself as she piled her fair hair up with tortoiseshell combs, and sprayed Shalimar at the base of her throat. She was looking forward to having supper with Roger in the garden. Not bad for sixty-one, she grinned at herself in the mirror and went lightly downstairs to wait for him.

Roger was whistling as he came through the front door. He had a roll of paper under his arm which he tossed onto the kitchen table.

'Supper's outside,' Anne called, 'it's still warm enough to eat in the garden, I think.'

'Excellent, excellent, I'll change and be out in a minute.'

Whatever he'd been doing in London had certainly improved his temper, Anne thought. She hoped he'd do it again.

He appeared five minutes later with a tray and the roll of paper. 'I've brought you a sherry, Anne,' he told her, unnecessarily. She could see it was sherry. Anne had hated sherry ever since she was pregnant with Emma, but either he never remembered, or took no notice.

'I'd much rather have a gin and tonic, Roger,' she said mildly.

He looked cross, and his face flushed red with annoyance. She knew he considered that to be *his* drink, but he just sighed and went back into the kitchen.

'Do wish you'd stop changing your mind about things, Anne,' he said as he placed what she found to be a very weak gin and tonic in front of her on the table.

'*Now* I'll tell you what I've been doing today.'

Anne fixed her blue eyes attentively on his face, and waited.

'We are to go to France.'

'Darling, that's lovely,' she breathed, 'I didn't know you'd been planning a holiday for us. Is it Frejus again or have you picked out somewhere different this time?' They had enjoyed several holidays over the years, both with the children and, after they'd grown-up, on their own. Anne loved Provence, with its bright light and the heady smell of marjoram and thyme which grew in profusion over the wooded hills.

'Oh no, Anne,' Roger said, smiling. 'Not just to holiday. To live.'

In the following weeks, she recalled that evening in detail. *Propriétés Française* held exhibitions for discerning buyers, he had told her, and there were only very few properties left in this desirable complex in Frejus, so they had to be quick.

She interrupted him. 'Complex? Do you mean a flat? We are to live in a flat?'

'Not a flat as *you* know it.' He unfolded the roll of paper and laid it on the table in front of her. 'They're apartments and very luxurious. It'll be wonderful Anne. Look here - there's the swimming pool and communal grounds - just think, no more weeding. You've got to face it old girl, you're not getting any younger.'

She shot him a look of pure dislike, but he flowed on regardless.

'We can have supper on our balcony and watch the sun go down over the Estorils; try out all the local wines, we can ...'

Anne held up her hand to cut him short. 'Exactly how far have you gone with this venture, Roger?' she asked him, 'and why haven't you told me before?'

'Knew you'd object unless I put it to you square on,' he said. 'Know how you hate change. Anyway, you'll have to sign a few things. You just have to trust me like you always do.'

'But I don't speak French, and yours isn't that good.'

'You'll learn when you're shopping - soon pick it up.'

'And what about the children?'

'They're not children any more, Anne. You should accept that now. Peter's in his first job and Emma's married with Suzie and Luke.'

'What about our grandchildren?' she came back at him. 'We'll miss them growing up, and Emma depends on me to help with the school run.'

'Exactly my point, Anne, everyone else has your attention and it's about time *I* had some. I feel that I've lost you along the way.'

Thrown by this unexpected emotional appeal, she said hopelessly, 'But Roger, we've already got a house. How can we afford this *luxurious* apartment?'

'Oh, we'll sell this house of course. Couldn't possibly have both.'

Her world was collapsing around her, and she would need all her experience to deal with it. She left matters there, with a sense of defeat that she'd never felt before.

The following evening, she poured herself an extremely large glass of Roger's gin and telephoned her children.

Emma exploded 'He can't possibly do this to you, Mum. It's absolutely ridiculous! What about your charities and the garden and - *us*?' Actually it's *such* bad timing because Dexters have offered me my old job back once Suzie starts school next month. I thought you could pick her up afterwards with Luke, and take them home for tea till I get back. I know you love having them.'

'You've got to hand it to Dad,' said Peter 'It's the first really cool thing he's ever done. Shame about the house, but it'll be great for us all to come and chill out round the pool.'

Her visit to Mrs Tufnell at Age Concern the following morning went along similar lines.

'Well, Mrs. Thornton, I must say I'm very surprised – you've always been so reliable. I'll be losing my best volunteer, and I depend on you when we go to San Repos for our month in the sun. So deserved, you'll agree?' She held up an ageing jersey for inspection. 'Now, is this gravy or something nastier?'

Liz said, 'Of course I'll miss you madly, but now you must decide what *you* want for a change.'

After talking to everyone, Anne thought about it for a long time. Except for Liz, they all had their own agenda, and it seemed that she was at the bottom of the list under 'Any Other Business.'

Apparently resigned to her fate, Anne got a last minute place at a Beginners' French class. 'Envy you going to live in Frejus, Mrs Thornton,' Doug Chapel, the tutor said. 'It's a beautiful, historic town, and I'm sure you'll pick up the language in no time. You've a natural ear, obviously well-used to listening to people,' he said.

'Yes, I've done a lot of that'

'Save a bed for me, then,' he said, and smiled.

'I certainly will,' she replied, and smiled in return.

One morning later that month, Anne confronted her husband. 'Could you please move your files off the dining room table, I've people coming today.'

'What people?' he snapped irritably.

'People who might buy the house. I told you about them yesterday.'

'Ah, well, that might be a bit precipitate,' he said, shifting uncomfortably from one foot to the other.

'In *what* way precipitate, Roger? And *do* use ordinary words, they're not going over a cliff, just buying a house.' She went on, 'I am so looking forward to our move after all. I've been on Google, and there's lots of expats living in Frejus, so many other English people we can be friends with. There's even a French-English boules team you can join. I'll offer English

Conversation classes in exchange for French - it'll be just like Brimley only with sun.' Anne turned to look at her husband who had gone very quiet. 'The files, Roger,' she reminded him gently. Later, she had been surprisingly compliant when Roger had voiced his doubts about the potential drawbacks to flat life. Always the possibility of neighbours who would want to chat in the communal grounds. Or swim, stroke for stroke with him in the rather tiny swimming pool discussing maintenance. Again, Anne had found it easier to agree with her husband, but this time she felt it was going to be a delightful compromise.

Their stone gite was cool after the heat of the day, but they were content to sit in the last of the evening sunlight on the paving stones outside the front door. They were eating s*alade nicoise* with the first of the lettuces from their garden. A half-drunk jug of cold wine sat on the table between them.

'I've been meaning to ask you,' Roger said lazily, 'what's with this French-English boules team? You know there's no such thing.'

'Oh, I made that up,' she replied

'*And* the English Conversation classes?'

'Those too, I'm afraid.'

'But it's such a good idea,' her husband said, 'Why don't you do it?'

'Would you join in?' Anne asked. 'We could do it together.'

'If I've time, but the new Archaeological digs are starting soon.'

'Shall we go back next month?' she asked.

'Best not. It's still school holidays – let them get the term well started.'

She noticed that they had both stopped calling it home.

173

'I thought I'd ask Doug Chapel out to stay – show off my French to him.'

'Great idea, Anne, if that's what you'd like?'

'Oh, I think I would like it very much.'

They smiled at each other and he poured her another glass of wine.

Eileen

Home at Last

He awoke with a start as he heard the key in the door. Now what? he thought drearily.

'Hallo, Dad! Where are you?'

'In here, Freddie.'

Freddie came into the sitting room. 'Why are you sitting in the dark? I thought you were out at first.'

Where did Freddie think he'd gone? Since he'd been widowed his life seemed to have closed in on him. He didn't like living on his own, having to do all the things Sarah used to do. Her illness and death had left him with little zest for life. He felt he couldn't be bothered to do anything anymore. 'Must have dozed off listening to my favourite Berlioz. Switch off the CD will you and we'd better have some lights. Join me in a sundowner?'

'Well, actually I've come to ask you to dinner, Dad. You haven't been round for days and Anne is worried that you aren't feeding yourself properly Anyway the kids would like to see their Grandpa. Come on, get your coat, it's cold out.'

'If you insist, but I'm quite happy here on my own.' He got up from his chair and followed his son through to the hall, where Freddie helped him on with his coat.

He caught his breath as he stepped out into the cold night air. Freddie held open the door of his Range Rover. His father hoisted himself up into the vehicle and they set off on the short journey to Freddie's home in the village.

'When did you get this car? All these dials and buttons; I couldn't be bothered with them myself,' he said, looking at the illuminated dashboard.

'Think it's about time you did change your old faithful for a newer model, Dad; an old classic or perhaps something nippy?'

'I'll get round to it one of these days, I suppose,' he replied listlessly.

Freddie pulled up in front of his home and, having helped his father out of the car, they entered the house together through the back door.

'Here we are, Anne. Dad is delighted to join us for dinner.'

'Hallo, Anne, good of you to ask me. How are you and where are those grandchildren of mine, young scamps?' Coming into the warm bright house, he felt a little better and during the evening he cheered up quite considerably.

When the time came to leave, Anne handed him a basket. 'I've made your favourite cake and there's a cottage pie for your lunch tomorrow. And don't leave it so long before you come and see us again.'

He promised he wouldn't, although he always waited to be invited. He didn't want to be a burden to his family. On the other hand, he wasn't looking forward to going back to his empty house.

On returning from taking his father home, Freddie decided something had to be done to help him. Freddie felt it was time to discuss the situation with his sister, Imogen.

'It's a bit late to call Italy, isn't it?' said Anne.

'Oh, she won't mind,' he replied as he dialled the number. 'Hello, Imogen! Sorry to call so late; always forget the time difference.'

Anne smiled at him and shook her head.

'The reason I'm calling is that we're worried about Dad,' he continued.

'He's not ill, is he?' Imogen asked anxiously.

'No, but he's very depressed and withdrawn these days; sits for hours listening to music in the dark. He hardly ever goes out and has stopped playing golf and going down to the local pub for a chat at lunchtime. We've suggested he gets a dog for company but he just seems to have lost interest in things generally.'

'I'm not surprised you're worried, Freddie. Not like Daddy at all, but we did notice that he was much quieter when we last visited. He is getting older and possibly his past is taking its toll. Perhaps he's just tired and, Freddie, he must be terribly lonely in that house without Mummy.'

'I know all that, Imogen, but we're really concerned. Even the kids don't cheer him up.'

'As it happens I need to come over to England and see my publisher. There's no rush but I'll make the arrangements as soon as possible and together we'll see if we can get Daddy interested in going forward.'

A few days later, Anne, Freddie and Imogen, who'd flown in from Italy that afternoon, visited their father.

'Oh, hallo everyone. What's this deputation about? How lovely to see you, Imogen. Are you staying long? How's the family?'

They trooped into the sitting room and Anne disappeared to prepare tea for everyone.

'It's good to be here. Just like old times, Daddy.' Imogen answered his questions and then said, 'Now, a question for you; what's this about your not going out much and not playing golf? You used to be the life and soul of things.'

'I don't know, Imogen. Anne and Freddie have been trying to get me motivated but I just don't seem to be able to get interested enough in anything. This little market town was an ideal place to live when I retired, so I thought, but when your Mother died it lost its charm.'

Anne came in with the tea tray and while she handed round the cups and plate of cakes, he continued.

'My childhood was spent travelling about and although I benefited in many ways, I never felt I belonged as I knew I would soon be off somewhere else. When I met your Mother, we were both very young. I felt that at last I could belong and put down roots but I had the wanderlust and spent my working life involved with pipelines, putting them together all over the world, as you know. I worked hard, played even harder and in the end settling down was just a dream. When I retired it was too late.' Would he ever overcome the guilt he felt? He'd let Sarah down. 'Your mother's illness caught up with us and she died.' He pulled his handkerchief from his trouser pocket and blew his nose, surreptitiously wiping his eyes at the same time. 'I should have retired earlier. It was selfish of me.'

'Oh, Dad, don't upset yourself. You know you gave Mum her dream here.'

'Too late, Freddie, too late!' he sighed.

Imogen crossed the room and sat on the arm of her father's chair. She took his hand and said, 'That's not true, Daddy. I believe that you and Mummy lived life to the full. Think of all the things that you did; the people you met; the places you've been. Freddie and I are very grateful for all the opportunities you gave us as children and we had a wonderful childhood. Mummy would want you to continue living the way you used to.'

'I'm too old, Imogen, to go back to the old lifestyle.'

'What is it that you miss most, Dad?'

'It's not so much the lifestyle, Freddie, it's the sun. Yes, the sun, the light and the way of life that goes with it. The energy one feels is missing here.'

'Well! You'll have to go to the sun! You'll be inundated with visitors, especially your family. Where would you like to go, Dad?'

His eyes brightened, 'Well, it's certainly worth thinking about and, as you say, everyone can visit and enjoy the sun with me.'

He went to bed that night with hope in his heart.

I'm so pleased that my children literally bullied me into taking a fresh look at my life and helped me to sell up and move here to Mallorca - my island in the sun. The warmth of the sun energises and revitalises me. I feel relaxed and have a sense of wellbeing once again. He smiles to himself.

A group of children run along the shore, a few yards in front of the verandah where he's sitting, followed, a few minutes later, by a young couple, arms entwined, caught up in their own world. Trailing behind them comes a woman carrying a pair of sandals in one hand, some floaty material blowing round her legs in the evening breeze. This is a new friend coming to call. Her name is Inez. He has known her for five weeks.

Am I going to be like Icarus and fly too close to the sun, he ponders? We cannot live without sunlight, so I will take the risk.

Life is too short.

Elaine

Grace Reef

'You won't regret this,' he said, eyes sparkling. This is the first day of the rest of my life, thought Antonio, as he looked round the store. He'd had a hard time since hurricane *Ivan, the Terrible* had whipped through Grenada, as had everyone. But now, three years on, things were better; tourists were coming back and he was looking forward to a busy time.

The lady he was addressing, smiled and nodded, 'I'd better not, Antonio. I'm depending on you.' She turned to leave. 'Best of luck for tomorrow,' she added.

Jean was English, a widow, in her late fifties but she kept herself fit and still had plenty of energy. She had been left very well off by her shipping magnate husband. This had stood her in good stead as the hotel she owned, on Grand Anse Beach, had suffered badly in the hurricane. The rebuild had taken time. Antonio had come to her rescue in restoring her beloved garden almost to its former glory. He and his team had worked long hours in sunshine and in rain; removing fallen trees, propping those which could be saved, clearing irrigation ditches, reseeding the damaged lawns, replacing broken plants. The lizards were back as were many of the small birds. In the past, visitors had come year after year to enjoy Jean's gardens. She was happily welcoming many of them back now the hotel was fully open.

Antonio was West Indian, good-looking, in his twenties with a fine physique. He was an excellent swimmer and he had become a well respected professional diving instructor. His dream of having his own dive centre had now come true, thanks to his patron. The only fly in the ointment was that, although he was fond of Jean, he felt she had feelings for him which were not exactly maternal and could spell disaster if he wasn't careful. Sometimes she was hostile to his friends and this made him wary of introducing them to her.

However, here he was. Smiling to himself, he wandered over to the racks where new equipment hung. Jean had been unstinting in the choice and quality, though he had been concerned about the cost. He looked at the range of BCDs (buoyancy control devices), and noted that the wetsuits were hanging according to size. He checked the gauges and regulators on the scuba tanks. The weight belts, masks, snorkels and fins, all the paraphernalia needed for scuba diving was stacked neatly ready for use. Yes, everything was ready for his first students arriving the next day.

He locked the centre, ran across the beach and dived into the sea. Swimming strongly, he reached his anchored motorboat and hauled himself aboard. Tomorrow, he thought, as he lay back in the sun, he would be taking his first tourists to a dive site. He closed his eyes, contented and happy. Life was good. He was looking forward to seeing Frances later that evening. She was a good diver; a little younger than Antonio.

He was thrilled she'd agreed to join him at the centre, though Jean had been less than enthusiastic when he'd told her. Jean, an experienced diver herself, was keen to assist Antonio, and made it obvious she didn't believe anyone else was needed. He hoped she would eventually accept Frances.

As the season progressed, Antonio became known for his excellent teaching and more tourists came to his dive centre. He showed them a video explaining the sport and then took them to the hotel swimming pool to practise scuba, before going out to sea. He and Frances worked well together and became closer. He moved out of the hotel to join her in her small flat overlooking the town, much against Jean's wishes. When he had large groups of divers, Jean joined them on the boat, but her attitude towards Frances didn't help and Antonio often had the unenviable task of smoothing troubled waters. He knew Frances wasn't one to accept Jean's acid comments silently.

Between dives there was much to be done, rinsing and checking equipment, refilling tanks and keeping the paperwork up to date. These tasks were often undertaken by Jean. However, Frances began to notice that her tanks weren't always filled properly and there were other small signs that her equipment was not being checked as thoroughly as it should. Once when she was teaching some guests in the swimming pool, she discovered the 'o' ring missing from the valve which meant the regulator wouldn't seal. This could have been a dangerous situation out at sea. Antonio queried why Frances insisted on going over everything herself before going out. She made excuses and eventually told Antonio she couldn't continue working with them because she'd lost her nerve. Antonio was devastated. He tried talking to her. He asked Jean if she knew what the trouble was; she just shrugged.

Their relationship didn't seem to be going anywhere and Antonio moved back into the hotel. He threw himself into his work and his business grew. He wanted to start repaying Jean but she wouldn't hear of it.

One day in early summer as they approached *Grace Reef,* an underwater sculpture of sixteen concrete and steel casts of Grenadian women, he and Jean noticed another vessel moving slowly over the area.

'What's happening, Joe?' Antonio shouted across the water to the skipper.

'We're installing a new sculpture,' came the reply, 'but you're welcome to take your divers to have a look.'

'Thanks, Joe,' replied Antonio and he and Jean began to prepare their divers, whilst their driver steered the motorboat in slow circles. Below them lay the Sculpture Park, designed and created by Jacob Ross. Once in the water the divers slowly descended in pairs to see the amazing creation.

Antonio was astonished to see Frances and her buddy working in the Sculpture Park. He dragged out his slate and wrote, 'C u later?' Frances gave the OK sign. She turned away but suddenly moved quickly towards Jean and her buddy. The man, on his first dive, was signalling *something is wrong*. Antonio saw Frances give Jean her alternative air supply and together they began to surface. He gestured to the other divers to follow. On the surface, he saw Frances checking Jean's breathing, and, instructing the other divers to get on board, he went over to them.

'I can't find a pulse,' yelled Frances.

'Quick, get her to the boat,' he shouted.

Frances's buddy joined them and they hauled Jean on board. Antonio shouted to his driver to take the divers back to shore, whilst Frances and her buddy took turns trying to resuscitate Jean. Antonio called the emergency services and the boat roared back to shore.

Jean took several weeks to recover. Antonio visited her frequently in hospital and later in her apartment at the hotel. Sometimes Frances accompanied him and he noticed that the enmity between the two women had diminished. They even teased him occasionally. The dive centre was investigated but when Jean tearfully admitted she had been advised to give up diving by her doctor months earlier, the case was dropped. Antonio was furious. He'd always insisted on everyone producing medical clearance before allowing them to try diving and here was his patron flouting the regulations.

'Don't be too hard on her,' urged Frances to Antonio's surprise, 'she's hating herself for causing so much trouble.'

Indeed the publicity had damaged Antonio's business. August came and went and the rainy season was soon in full swing often bringing poor visibility for diving.

'Let's go away for a while, Antonio,' suggested Frances. 'We can come back in time for the Christmas rush. The weather will be better then and all this will probably be forgotten.'

'Good idea. But first we need to set up an advertising campaign for the dive centre, if we want some work during the winter. Then I fancy New England in the Fall. What say you?'

'Great, I'll get on the Internet straight away and see what flights I can find. We'll hire a car and explore,' said Frances, smiling.

Antonio wanted to include her in his plans for the dive centre. He loved her very much and the break might give them time to get back together again.

Jean waved them goodbye with relief. She was feeling old and foolish. Why had she ever dreamt this young man could be interested in her? How badly she had treated Frances and now she had jeopardised Antonio's business by her stupid behaviour.

How could she make it up to them? She was too busy catching up with her work in the hotel for the first week they were away to give it much thought. Then she turned her attention to the surprise she had in mind for their return.

'Come aboard,' She called as Frances and Antonio got out of the taxi she'd sent to the airport to collect them.

Mystified, the two climbed on to the deck of the catamaran, *Shadowfax*. It was a warm evening; lights were coming on around the harbour. Jean passed them glasses of champagne and then opened the saloon door. Roars of laughter came from the crowd inside and their friends erupted on to the deck.

Jean held up her glass, 'Here's to you both and welcome home,' she cried.

'To Frances and Antonio,' they chorused.

'What's all this in aid of?' laughed Antonio, as the captain started the engine and cast off.

'Wait and see,' smiled Jean.

The vessel made its way out of the harbour and along the coast towards her hotel. From some distance, Frances and Antonio could make out the dive centre below the hotel. The beach suddenly exploded into lights of many colours. Smells from a barbecue drifted towards them and a steel band struck up as they drew near. *Shadowfax* came to rest on the beach and everyone leapt from the boat into the warm surf and made their way ashore.

'Help yourselves,' said Jean and they moved towards the barbecue and tables laden with salads and drinks.

'What a home-coming, Jean,' exclaimed Frances later that evening. 'Thank you, thank you.'

Antonio put his arm round Jean's shoulders, 'Thank you,' he said quietly.

'Now just a minute,' replied Jean. She gestured to the band to stop playing and took a deep breath, 'Listen everyone, I have an announcement to make. As you know, I owe my life to this young lady.' She gave Frances a squeeze. 'And,' turning to Antonio, 'this young man has put up with an old woman for long enough.'

Antonio shook his head.

'No, let me finish. He brought my garden back to life after hurricane *Ivan*. I'm going to concentrate on my gardening from now on and I wish Antonio and Frances to do the same with the dive centre. So today I am giving it to them as equal partners.'

'Oh, Jean, that's so generous,' cried Antonio.

Frances gasped and hugged them both. Antonio whispered, 'Is this going to be more than a business partnership, Frances?'

She blushed and nodded vigorously. Jean smiled broadly and once again their friends raised their glasses, this time, to the three of them.

Eve

 *Finis*